20

THE GIRLS OF CANBY HALL

FRIENDS TIMES THREE

EMILY CHASE

SCHOLASTIC INC.
New York Toronto London Auckland Sydney

For Katharine Stilwell Carey

ISBN 0-590-40392-3

12 11 10 9 8 7 6 5 4 3 2 1   7 8 9/8 0 1 2/9

Printed in the U.S.A.   01

First Scholastic printing, February 1987

THE GIRLS
OF CANBY HALL

FRIENDS
TIMES THREE

THE GIRLS
OF CANBY HALL

CHAPTER ONE

Andrea Cord flew across the campus of Canby Hall to her dorm, Baker House, where she shared Room 407 with Jane Barrett and Toby Houston. It was almost impossible to believe that the first term was almost over and that vacation was about to begin. It seemed like only yesterday that she'd first come to Canby Hall and met Jane and Toby, and tomorrow she was already going home for the Christmas/New Year break.

Home to Andrea was Chicago, Illinois. It was the comfortable, big apartment she shared with her parents and her two brothers and baby sister in the city's middle-class, racially mixed neighborhood. It was her family's restaurant, Steak 'n Ribs, where everyone in the family pitched in. It was the Chicago Ballet where, one day, she hoped to dance.

Andy pirouetted in joy before she hopped up the steps and into the dorm. She pulled off

1

a woolen hat and smoothed her black hair.

As she entered the building, her next-door neighbor, Maggie Morrison, was leaving. "Andy," Maggie said, "your dad called a little while ago."

"Probably just couldn't wait until I get home tomorrow afternoon," Andy replied, laughing.

"I guess that's right," Maggie said. "Anyway, he's going to call again in half an hour. I'm sure we can set our watches by it."

It was an ongoing joke in Baker House that when Andy had left for school, she hadn't been homesick, her family had been *Andy*-sick. She loved everyone in her family with all her heart, but she knew that it was good for everyone to have a little relief from their closeness. Still, she was really looking forward to vacation.

But first, there was a small celebration for the roommates of 407.

"Party time!" Jane announced when Andy opened the door. Since Jane's last class had been at noon, she'd gone into town and purchased the goodies. As soon as Andy's coat was in the closet, Jane handed her a soft drink and opened the box of cookies she'd bought.

Andy watched while Jane, pretty with long blond hair and sparkling blue eyes, struggled to make a space to sit on her bed. She shifted a pile of clothes, creating a small clearing. Andy shook her head. Jane always had a pile of clothes on her bed — *expensive* clothes.

"Just think, Jane. Only one more day and you'll be back home in Boston where the maid will pick up your clothes for you. Which is it? Upstairs maid or downstairs maid?"

"Upstairs," Jane answered without hesitation and then laughed. She knew she was a slob, seemingly unrepentant. Her compromise with her roommates was to keep her mess in her third of the room. It worked most of the time.

October Houston, Toby for short, sat on her own bed, solemnly drinking her soda. Toby's close-cropped red curls framed an oval face with deep green eyes. In contrast to her chatty roommates, Toby was the quiet one. Raised by her father on a ranch in Texas, she frequently found it easier to talk to horses than people, but after three months with Andy and Jane, she was beginning to understand the appeal of civilization — in small doses.

"A penny for your thoughts, Toby," Andy said.

"Oh, I don't think they're worth that much. I was just looking at the snow on the ground and thinking that I won't be seeing any more of that until after we get back here in two weeks."

"Seventeen days," Andy corrected her. "See, it's two weeks plus an extra weekend. And that means an extra weekend of ballet performances for me. You know who is doing *The Nutcracker?* Oh, and yeah, there's going to be a special performance by the — "

"Yes, Andy," Jane interrupted. "You've told us. We know about the tickets you've managed to get. I'm looking forward to Christmas, but I wish I were looking forward to the rest of the vacation the way you are. Things are actually going to be kind of boring in Boston, depending on how you feel about tea parties — not the kind where you dress up as an Indian and throw tea into the harbor — the fund-raising kind. That's what Mother is specializing in this vacation."

"What you mean is that it'll be boring because Cary is going skiing in Colorado, don't you Jane?" Toby asked.

"Well, there's that, too," Jane admitted. Cary Slade was the one really offbeat thing about Jane. Most of her life was pretty staid — her clothes, her taste in music, art, and friends. Then there was Cary, lead guitarist in the punk-rock group, Ambulance.

"I wish Ambulance had gotten a gig in Boston instead of Colorado for the vacation, but it's a great opportunity for Cary. So what if I suffer?"

"It's not all that bad, Jane," Toby comforted her. "Remember, Cary will be here when you come back. It's only two weeks — pardon me, seventeen days — without him. Now in my case, it's a little bit different. Here I've been in snowy Massachusetts for three months, terribly homesick for my Dad. He'll be there when I get home, but right after

Christmas he's got to go to a stock ranchers' convention and I can't go with him. I know I'll have a good time riding my horse Max — if he remembers me — but there I'll be in Texas, homesick for Dad. I may even miss you two."

Jane decided to break the gloomy mood that was settling in on the trio. "Cheer up, girls. Let's start the party. First things first. Let's get down to presents." She was beaming so proudly that both Andy and Toby knew she had good ones for them.

Ceremoniously, Jane handed each a beautifully wrapped package — each large and flat. Andy opened hers first. From years of training, she carefully preserved the wrapping paper, not tearing even where the tape was. When the last of the paper was folded back, she could barely speak. Her gift was a beautifully framed reproduction of a Degas painting of ballet dancers — a much better reproduction than any she had ever seen.

"Hey, we had a five-dollar limit on presents, Jane. You didn't do this for five bucks!"

"Sure I did. It didn't cost me anything. That painting was in Grandfather's collection — now part of the art museum. I just called the curator and asked if she could do me a favor. Mother has never turned me down in the past. She didn't this time, either."

"I love it, Jane! Thank you," Andy told her.

"You're welcome, Andy. Now you, Toby," Jane said.

Carefully, Toby removed the paper from hers. She was almost unable to speak, but her face glowed. It was a reproduction of a Remington pen-and-ink drawing of a cattle drive. "Grandfather collected Remingtons, too?"

"He was a man of wide-ranging interests," Jane said.

"Yes and his granddaughter inherited his good taste," Toby said, setting her gift aside long enough to give Jane a hug. Andy joined her.

Jane was a little embarrassed by the enthusiastic thanks. "Now listen, all this doesn't come for nothing, you know. You guys have some stuff for me, don't you?"

"Oh, yeah, sure," Andy teased. "But it's not from my grandfather's collection! Okay, here goes." She handed a small package to each.

Toby opened hers first. It was a mug with a map of Texas on one side and a longhorn steer on the other. Inside, on the bottom, was a Lone Star.

"I love it, Andy. How did you get a Texas cup up here in Massachusetts?"

"Oh, I have my sources," Andy evaded, not wanting to mention the church bazaar she'd attended. "Besides, I thought it was real important to have a tea cup for that tea bag you've got." All three looked slyly at the ceiling over Toby's bed where a teabag was suspended, just as it had been since the first day of school when Toby had put it there. Everybody wanted to know what it was for. But Toby just smiled a secret smile.

"What a good idea," she said. "It's just great. As a matter of fact, I think I'll have my next cup of tea in this lovely cup."

Then it was Jane's turn to open a package. She tore away the paper and dropped the shreds on the floor. It had been very hard for Andy to think of just the right thing for Jane. After all, Jane could afford anything she wanted.

"Huh?" Jane said, holding the unwrapped can in her hand. It was all Andy could do to keep from laughing while Jane read the label on the electric-blue aerosol can.

"Hair-Blu?" Jane asked.

Then she understood. Andy had given her a can of spray-on hair color — in this case electric blue. "Hey, neat!" Jane said, delighted. "It's for when I go to punk concerts with Ambulance, isn't it?" Andy and Toby nodded between giggles.

"Great — just what Cary would like — and while he's in Colorado, I can wow the Ladies' Auxiliary at their tea parties!" The image of rather proper Jane going to a fund-raising tea with electric-blue hair was too much — even for Jane.

"I don't know, Andy," Jane said between giggles. "Maybe I'd just better leave it here for the vacation, so temptation doesn't overwhelm my better sense." They laughed in agreement.

"Okay, Toby, it's your turn now," Andy said. Shyly, Toby removed two packages from under her bed.

"It was hard, you know. You two are so different from any friends I've ever had. I just didn't know what you might like, but I thought maybe a little bit of Texas would be good for each of you." She handed the identical packages to Andy and Jane. They opened them together. Inside each, was a hand-tooled leather wallet and change purse.

"I hope you like them," Toby told her friends nervously. "It's real Texas leather. You see there's a hand on the ranch who does this work in his spare time and I thought — "

"Toby, it's *beautiful*," Andy said, admiring the intricate work on the leather.

"I never had anything like it," Jane told her, loving the pungent smell. "You must have noticed that my old one was falling to pieces, didn't you?"

"Well, actually, I did. I know you had one of those French designer things, but this kind is really handy — and more durable. Look, there's even a place for your credit cards, Jane," Toby showed her.

"I hope there's no place for *my* credit cards, Toby," Andy teased. "After all, there's only one person in this room with credit cards."

"Don't worry, Andy," Toby comforted her. "That good, strong Texas cowhide will last a lifetime. You'll have lots of credit cards before it wears out."

"In the meantime, I've got a library card," Andy pointed out. And with that, she began transferring things from her old wallet to her new one. "It's just great, Toby. Thank you very much. You're right, too. Now we all have just a little bit of Texas with us all the time."

"Time for seconds on soda," Jane announced, pouring some into her cup. "And then we pack to return to civilization. We're all taking the 8:17 train to Boston in the morning, aren't we? And then, by the time you guys get to the airport, well, I guess, the upstairs maid will have unpacked my suitcases and the downstairs maid will have shined my shoes and the midstairs maid will have — "

She couldn't go on. The pillows that bombarded her made it very difficult to talk.

Suddenly, Jane sat up straight. "Hold it! How could I forget? Your father called, Andy. He said he'd call back, but he sounded kind of upset. I think he'll feel better if you call him."

"Thanks, that's a good idea. Maggie mentioned that he'd call when I was coming in," Andy said, standing up to go to the phone booth down the hall. Canby Hall students could get calls on their room phones, but couldn't make them. "He probably just can't wait the next twenty hours until I'm home. You know, when Andysickness sets in, who you gonna call?"

Jane and Toby could see that Andy really was eager to make the call. No matter how much of a bother her family was sometimes, it was always nice to be loved like that. While Andy was out, they picked up the party things and threw out the garbage — once Toby had set the example for Jane. Then Jane helped Toby hang her Remington print on the wall next to her bed.

"Jane, I hope you know how much this means to me," Toby said.

"I'm glad," Jane told her. "You know, it wasn't easy for me to get presents good enough for the two of you, either."

Toby knew that she learned more about friendship from her roommates than she had all the previous sixteen years of her life. Suddenly vacation seemed very long. She concentrated on her packing.

"Oh, no!" were the first words out of Andy's mouth when she returned to the room. "I can't believe it!"

"Is something wrong?"

"Everything is wrong," Andy said. She flopped onto her bed dejectedly and buried her face in her hands. "Everything."

CHAPTER TWO

W hat is it?" Toby asked.

"It's my vacation," Andy sighed. "I mean, it's over. All the ballet, all the theater. None of it's going to happen now."

Toby and Jane looked at each other, mystified.

"What are you talking about?" Jane asked.

"It's Robert and Elaine, don't you see?"

No, they didn't.

"I think you're going to have to explain this from the start," Toby suggested sensibly.

"I guess so," Andy said, sniffing, but pulling herself together. "Robert and Elaine are Dad's very best waiter and waitress. Dad always says that each of them does the work of three. Customers love them and often come to our restaurant just because the service is so good. Well, the worst thing happened: Elaine and Robert fell in love!"

"What's so bad about that? I mean, doesn't

11

everyone want to fall in love?" Jane asked.

"Sure, but they've gone and gotten married!" Andy wailed in explanation.

"Andy, what *is* going on here?" Jane demanded. "You are not making any sense at all." She spoke very firmly.

"No, I guess I'm not. Okay, so Elaine and Robert have gotten married — they've *eloped* — and tomorrow, they are leaving for their honeymoon in Jamaica."

"So nice and warm this time of year," Jane said brightly. "Say, maybe they'll meet up with Alison and David. That's where they are going on their honeymoon." Alison was Baker House's beloved housemother. She'd been married at Thanksgiving to David, a newscaster from Boston. They were taking a delayed honeymoon over the Christmas vacation. "Oh, that sounds wonderful!"

Andy knitted her brows. "Well, to you that sounds wonderful, and to Elaine and Robert and Alison and David that sounds wonderful, but to *me*, it sounds like I'm going to have to do all their work. It's just about impossible to hire reliable people at this time of year, and Dad doesn't like to have to train strangers for short-term jobs. The good news is that business is so good Dad's got banquets booked every night I'm going to be home. The bad news is that I'm going to have to work at them."

"Can't you just say no?" Jane asked.

"No way, Jane. It isn't like having a maid

to pick up after you. When you're running a family restaurant, the whole family pitches in. Those blue-plate specials are paying my tuition, and I've got to carry my weight. I just wish it weren't so. So, farewell, *Nutcracker; adieu, Romeo and Juliet; auf Wiedersehen, Swan Lake*. Hello, sirloin steak; hold the vegetables; light on the gravy — oh, and can you make that well-done?" Andy sat bleakly on the edge of her bed.

"Well, it sounds like all three of us are going to have boring vacations," Jane said.

"Mine won't be boring," Andy assured her. "It just isn't going to be what I had in mind — at all."

Then, there was a knock at the door. Maggie Morrison stuck her head in.

"Can Dee and I come in?" Maggie and Dee shared Room 409, next to 407. Maggie and Dee were opposites that attracted. Maggie was a New Yorker, skinny with big glasses and dark hair. Dee was from California, beach country, blond with a perfect figure. Maggie's idea of proper dress was a striped cotton skirt, flowered shirt, wide belt and shoes to match. Dee's was a string bikini, surfboard to match. They were two of the most popular girls in school, and for good reason. They were also two of the nicest and friendliest girls in school.

"Welcome to Glum Chums," Andy invited.

"What's got you guys down?" Dee asked.

"Yeah," Maggie said. "Just a few minutes ago, unless my ears deceived me, you were all howling with laughter about something. What did we hear in the high decibel area, Dee, 'Hair-Blu'?"

"Well, that was funny a few minutes ago, but now all we can think of is how miserable we're all going to be the second week of vacation."

"I had the same problem," Maggie said. "Mom is working and Dana is in Hawaii."

"Me, too," Dee said. "I was going to be stuck with miles and miles of sandy beach and nobody to share it with."

"So," Maggie explained. "I agreed to go to Malibu from New York where I'll be with my Mom for Christmas. That way, I get family time, but not too much, and I have some time with friends, too."

"A lot of friends, Maggie," Dee said, almost threateningly. They giggled. Dee's ability to collect friends around her was almost a legend at Canby Hall. In fact, she had been so convincing about the joys of surfing and sand that she'd gotten everyone on the fourth floor of Baker House to have a surfing party. There was still plenty of sand in the corners of the shower room to attest to the party's success. Nobody would ever tell the cleaning staff how it got there.

All the cheer was getting to Andy. "That's just fine for *you*," she said. "But we three can't exactly drop everything and come to Malibu — friends or no. Well, actually, Toby and Jane probably could. It's just me who would be stuck beneath a giant tray of 'tonight's specials'."

"Say, Jane and Toby," Dee began. "If you want to come out to Malibu, I'm sure it'd be okay — "

"Uh, Dee," Maggie interrupted. "I think there's something else brewing here."

Andy was really getting into her funk. "Jane and Toby, I think Malibu may be the answer to your problems. You can go and get sun and surf and meet all those wonderful boys who keep calling Dee all the time and have all the fun. That's the answer to your problem. Me? I can't get to the ocean. I can't even get to *Swan Lake*. There *is* no answer to my problem."

Then Jane spoke. "You know, Andy, you might have something."

"You're going to go to Malibu?"

"No, not Malibu. Say, Toby, do you have a direct flight from Boston to San Antonio?"

"No, it's easier to go through Denver or Chicago, so I go through Chicago."

"Do you have a layover there on your way back?" Jane asked.

"I guess it's about an hour. I think Andy's on the same Chicago-to-Boston return flight with me."

"Could you make it a longer layover?" Jane asked.

Then Toby began to see the light. "You mean about seven days?" Toby said.

"Something like that," Jane said.

"Hmmm. What about you?" Toby asked slyly.

"I think I could talk Mother into a trip to Chicago."

"Why would your mother want to come to Chicago?" Andy asked, still confused.

"It's not my mother who would travel. *I* would," Jane said.

"I don't get it," said Andy.

"I can tell you don't get it," Jane said. "As I see it, your Dad is short two people. He's expecting you to fill their shoes. There's no getting around that. So, *Swan Lake* is drained. Still, there *is* a way to make your work load lighter."

"What's that?"

"Hire two other people."

"Are you crazy?" Andy said. "Who?"

"At your service," Jane said gracefully, bowing from the waist. Toby followed suit.

"You mean you two would give up your vacations to come work at Dad's restaurant?"

"Those fun-filled, laugh-a-minute, social-whirlwind vacations we have planned? You bet we'd give them up for you!" Toby assured her.

For the first time in ten minutes, Andy stopped frowning. She was thinking. Hard.

Jane, Toby, Dee, and Maggie all watched in silent expectation. Soon, a smile crept across Andy's lips and then her eyes were twinkling and then she was laughing.

"You are just crazy, wonderful friends.

That's the nicest offer anyone could ever make. I can't tell you how great it is and I know you think you really mean it. I'm already happy just thinking about what great friends I have. When you back out, I'll still think you're great friends."

"We're not backing out, Andy," Jane said.

"No way!" Toby agreed.

"Really?"

"Really!" Toby and Jane said in one voice.

"Wait a minute," Andy said, now sounding doubtful. "This is nice as nice can be, and now I know you're really sincere, but what does either of you know about waitressing?"

The roommates were silent for a while, thinking.

"I've worked in the mess hall at the ranch," Toby offered. "It can't be too different from being a waitress. I mean, the guys tell you how much they want on their plates and you try to get it all on without mixing the beans into the mashed potatoes. Then, when they complain about the food, you ignore it. Do we have to do any more than that?"

Andy started laughing at the image of her Dad's nice little restaurant being a cowboy dining room, slopping food on plates to overflowing, turning a deaf ear to complaints.

"Well, Toby, actually, if you ever want to see the customers again, it's usually recommended to listen politely when people complain in your restaurant — "

"I know," Toby assured her. "I was just

teasing. Actually, I did work in a diner near the high school one semester. It's hard work, but I learned something about it."

"And you?" Andy asked Jane. "Don't tell me you've worked in a diner."

"No, of course not, but I've certainly seen my mother train enough maids. I know you serve from the left and clear from the right. And I've served a *lot* of tea."

Andy had to admit that that was more than she'd known her first day working at the restaurant as a waitress. "Think you could learn to balance a tray on one hand?"

"Can you?" Jane asked.

"Sure," Andy told her.

"Then show me how you do it. I'm sure I could learn."

"Okay, I'll show you." Andy's eyes searched the room for something to serve as a tray. She spotted a tray filled with jewelry on Jane's bureau. "Here, give me that."

Removing the jewelry, Jane handed it to her.

Andy balanced it on her right hand, palm up. "Now, I need something to carry — like to pretend they're plates."

"How about some cups?" Jane suggested, offering her empty cup. Toby offered hers, too.

Carefully, Andy placed the cups on the tray.

"See, you have to be careful how you distribute the plates. You want the weight to be even or the whole thing will tip. Here we go." Andy lifted the tray carefully to shoulder height, elbow forward, edges balanced by resting on her right shoulder. "This is all there is to it," she told her friends and began walking through the room as if through a restaurant.

"Let me try," Jane said. She took the tray from Andy and, slowly, slowly, started to walk.

For a while, the cups remained motionless, steady and still on the tray. Soon, however, they began a forward movement, slipping toward the front edge.

"Sometimes, the load seems to shift," Andy explained. "Then all you have to do is to adjust the level with your left hand."

Jane raised the front of the tray. The cups slid backwards to the rear edge.

"Sometimes, you overcompensate, though, so you try, real hard, to shift the load to the center again," Andy said.

Jane's left hand brought the front end down and the tilt brought the cups tumbling down off the tray.

"I think you dropped something," Andy said.

"Like three orders of spaghetti, two steaks, and an eggplant special, right?" Toby teased.

"One of the most important things to know is that even the most experienced serving person will really blow it every now and again," Andy said.

"I'll keep that in mind," Toby told her.

"Me, too," Jane said. "And now we know how to do it. Next, you can teach us how *not* to do it."

"That'll be Lesson Two," Andy told them.

"You know, I bet I really could teach you two to be top-notch waitresses. Maybe — just maybe — this will work. Of course, convincing me is easy. It's Dad who will be the final judge. I think I'll call him now."

Andy slipped out of the room to the telephone booth in the hall.

"Can't be all that hard, can it?" Dee asked.

"Are you kidding?" Maggie countered. "Being a waitress is very hard work. Exhausting. There are a lot of tricks to it, too. I mean, you think all you're doing is carrying food, but you're really a very important part of how much the people enjoy their dinner."

"But it can't be all that hard to learn, can it?" Dee asked again.

"Probably no harder than surfing," Toby suggested.

That hit home. "No harder than surfing? Do you have any idea how hard surfing can be? I mean, anybody can hold on to a board that's floating toward a beach, but if you're going to hang ten in the pipeline, why it takes a lot of training, even — "

"That's the point, then, isn't it?" Toby interrupted. "I mean *any*body can slop food onto a plate, but if you're going to be a good waitress, it can take a lot of training. Jane, do you have any idea what we've gotten ourselves into?"

"None at all," Jane assured her. "I just know that Andy needs our help and we're going to give it to her — if it kills us."

"It may," Maggie said ominously. "Get yourselves some comfortable shoes. Come on, Dee, let's pack. Have a great vacation!" Maggie and Dee waved good-bye and left for their room.

Down the hall, in the phone booth, Andy spoke. "Of course you know who they are, Dad. . . .

"Well, sure, I know they won't be much help, at least at first. . . .

"No, I can train them. . . .

"Well, I'll start now, Dad. I can tell them what they need to know. . . .

"Right, I told you. They've both had some experience waitressing. Well, not exactly waitressing. I mean they've both worked with sort of, uh, related things. . . .

"Like a cowboy dining room. . . .

"Well, they serve food there. She even told me she knows how to handle complaints. . . .

"And the other? Uh, well, she's been directly involved in an ongoing waitress training program. . . .

"Run by her mother, Dad — *that's* who runs it. . . .

"Not exactly a school, but I guess, well, sort of. . . .

"I know I told you she doesn't pick up her clothes, but she'll certainly pick up dirty dishes. . . .

"Because she's my friend. . . .

"The other one, too. . . .

"Come on, Dad, give them a chance. I mean, you know how much this vacation meant to me. It seems the least you could do for me. Isn't it? . . .

"Yeah, Dad, it would mean a lot to have them there. . . .

"Steve Palmer will be there? . . .

"Well, I'm glad there's going to be at least one other seasoned server. Sure they can work with him. So can I. . . .

"Please, Dad — " There was a long silence.

"You're wonderful, Daddy. Believe me, you won't be sorry. I love you and Mom a bunch and a half. I'll see you tomorrow. . . .

"Good-night to you, Dad."

Triumphant, she returned to Room 407.

CHAPTER THREE

Toby was in the stable saddling her horse,
Max, when she heard her father's voice
ring out across the yard.

"Toby! The phone's for you! It's Madam
Boston again."

Again was right, Toby laughed to herself.
This was the third phone call she'd had from
Jane since she'd gotten back home to Texas.
Still, it was nice to have a girl friend care
enough to call — and call.

"Tell her I'll be right there, Dad."

Toby smoothly slipped the bit into Max's
soft mouth and slid the bridle over his ears,
buckling it gently. She gave him a reassuring
pat on his shoulder and climbed out of the
stall. She jogged over to the extension telephone by the stable door.

"Howdy," she drawled into the phone.

"Oh, Toby, you've only been home a week
and you sound so *Texas*."

"It's the horsey influence, I guess. I'm in the stable."

"Okay, well, you stay there for just a minute. I'm going to get Andy on the line."

The phone went silent while Jane manipulated her father's office telephone system to create a conference call among the three roommates. After a short while, she heard Andy's familiar voice.

"Hi, Toby. Are you really in the stable? I mean, like, are there horses around you?"

"Sure thing!" Toby told her.

"Now listen," Jane broke in sensibly. "We've got to make plans or something could go very wrong. Here's the scoop on the airplane tickets and arrivals. . . ."

Jane explained exactly what had been going on with the travel plans. As far as Toby was concerned, that didn't matter. All she had to know was what plane to take, the rest would work. Toby was always amused, and she suspected her roommates were as well, by the vast differences among them. Just now, for instance, Andy was amazed by the fact that Toby was surrounded by horses; Toby was amazed by the fact that Jane could use a phone to call two people at the same time; Jane was amazed by the fact that Andy had a job and it was important to her family.

"Jane, you're going to have to learn this waitressing stuff," Andy said.

"All right, then you'd better tell me again," Jane said.

"It's really simple. You just listen for your signal."

"How do I know it's *my* signal?"

"Because each of us has a different chime sequence. Like mine is da-dee-da. Yours will probably be dee-dee-da, maybe da-da-dee, or else that will be Toby's. Anyway, when you hear it, you know your order is ready."

"How do I know which order it is?" Jane asked.

"Because it's written down on the little pad, the one you'll use to add the bill. It's got the table number on it."

"How do I know which table is which number?" Jane went on.

"I'll *tell* you which is which." Andy sounded weary.

Jane was really very anxious about her foray into the working world. She wasn't afraid of work. She never had been. In fact, she was a very hard worker. She worked hard at school and had worked hard as a volunteer at the art museum the summer before. She'd just never done anything like being a waitress. That was what other people did — people you hired.

"How do I know who ordered which item?" Jane went on determinedly.

"*Jane,* you write it on the bill in the order they give it to you and you make a note which person ordered first. If you get confused, you can always ask 'Who ordered the calf's liver?' "

"Yuck! Calf's liver?"

"Oh, yeah, and the one really important

thing I forgot to tell you. Don't *ever* say 'yuck'
when somebody orders something you don't
like."

Toby spoke then. "How about 'bleah'? Is
that okay?"

"Much better," Andy told them solemnly,
before they all started laughing too hard to
speak.

It amazed Andy how little her friends knew
about her life. Sure, they knew all about Andy
at Canby Hall, but that was only a small part
of her. She wondered, and worried a bit, how
they would feel about her whole family; if
they'd like the restaurant; if they'd decide she
was too strange. It wasn't even a matter of her
being black. She knew that didn't mean anything to her friends. It was that she was different from them in other ways and always
had been. But then, she thought, they were
different from each other, too, and she
wouldn't be worried if she were going to
Toby's house, or Jane's. Not much, anyway.

Finally, she decided she was being silly. Her
two best friends were coming to bail her out
of a rotten situation at her family's restaurant
and, really, she couldn't wait until they
arrived.

"How's your father feeling about us today,
Andy?" Jane asked.

"On again," she said. She didn't tell them
that yesterday he'd been "off again."

"That's a relief, since we'll be there in three
days."

"It's a relief to me, too," Andy assured her friends. "This time, I'm sure it's going to stick." Andy recalled how her father had wavered about her friends coming to pitch in. "The thing that finally brought him around was when I told him you'd bring fresh live lobsters from Boston."

"It seems like the least I can do since I'm coming for such a long vacation visit," Jane said graciously.

Vacation? Once again, Andy was a little anxious about Jane's notion of her trip to Chicago.

"Jane," Toby cut in. "I hardly think this will be a holiday."

"Well, you know what I mean — a working vacation."

"You're going to work for those tips, Jane," Andy said.

"We'll get tips?" Jane asked.

"Sure you will. Unless you *do* say 'yuck' when guests order liver."

"I promise I won't. I'll just say it if they order pea soup."

"That'll help a lot," Andy said, laughing. "Oh, one other thing I ought to mention — "

"Yeah?" Toby and Jane said together.

"It's twenty below zero here today. And with the windchill factor — "

"Don't tell us!" Toby cut her off.

"That's right. I'm sure you don't want to know anyway. But bring warm clothes."

"I'll bring the best I've got. But if it's not

good enough, we can go to Marshall Field's,"
Jane replied.

Andy shook her head in amazement. Jane
was Jane and that's all there was to it. "Sure,
Jane. You have an account there?"

"No. But I can use my mother's."

Yes, Jane was Jane.

"Okay, then, I'll see you both on Monday
at O'Hare Airport. Toby gets in at 2:45; Jane
arrives at 3:10. We should be able to get to
the restaurant in time for the early diners.
Can't wait until then."

"Me, neither. This is going to be fun," Jane
said.

"Interesting," Toby added.

"Right. Merry Christmas until then," Andy
said.

"Yeah. Merry Christmas," Toby agreed.

"Good-bye."

"Good-bye."

"Bye-bye."

Toby hung up the phone and pushed the
stable door open to lean against one of the
wooden beams that framed the entrance to
the stable. She stared out across the plains
where her father's cattle grazed. A stiff breeze
whipped the grass.

She turned to finish saddling Max so she
could go for a long ride in the bright winter
sunshine. She wondered what the windchill
factor was in Chicago. But, as she thought
back over the phone conversation, she had the

uneasy feeling that cold weather could be the least of the problems in Chicago. Stop it! she thought. They were going there to *solve* problems, not cause them, and she would see that that's what happened. Besides, they almost always had a lot of fun together.

This would be no exception. She hoped.

CHAPTER FOUR

Jane was just a little bit frantic.

She had an hour and a half to get to the airport, but she figured she had at least two hours worth of packing to do. And it would take her forty minutes to get to the airport.

She pawed through her drawers, pulling out everything she thought she might possibly need, but she didn't really know. After all, she'd never been to Chicago alone before — and she'd never been a waitress before. How could she pack for the unknown?

Jane, you're being silly, you know, she told herself. Then she sat down on the bed and started laughing at herself. She *was* being silly and it was funny. Basically, what she was doing was going to a city a little colder than her own to visit a friend and to help out at her friend's family's restaurant. Surely her wardrobe could cover that.

She looked critically at the giant stack of

clothes in her suitcase and dumped them back onto her bed. With new resolve, she began again, this time selecting a reasonable group of warm, casual clothes and one slightly dressy outfit, just in case. The black velvet sheath and the pink lace dress she'd worn to Charlotte's debutante party went back in the closet.

It didn't take her two hours to pack. In fact, it only took about fifteen minutes and left her plenty of room for her makeup and shampoo.

She paused for a moment, reflecting on possible omissions. Then, sure she was finished packing, she closed and zipped the bag, and put on her coat to leave for the airport. As she was about to turn out the light in her room, she glanced at the stack of leftover clothes she'd left on her bed. With new resolve, she set her coat on top of her suitcase and spent the five minutes necessary to tidy the mess she'd left. Toby and Andy would be proud of her, she thought.

"I'm very sorry, Miss Barrett," the man at the check-in counter told her. "There's been a mix-up with reservations and I'm afraid there's nothing I can do at this point. I do not have any other seats in First Class for this flight. I'd be pleased to put you on the next available flight to Chicago in First Class, or we can give you Coach accommodations on this flight. If you select that option, I'm authorized to give you three First Class 'upgrades' for future flights. That means you'll be able to buy Coach tickets, but fly First Class."

Jane shrugged. "It really doesn't matter," she said. "Coach is fine with me. It was just that my father's travel agent automatically orders — Did you say *three* First Class upgrades?"

The man nodded. Suddenly Jane could picture how much fun she and Andy and Toby would have traveling First Class together on their way back to school.

"I'll take that, please."

"Thank you, Miss Barrett," the man said, quickly filling out the necessary forms for Jane.

Jane glanced at her seat assignment — 18A. There had to be some mistake. For in 18B was just about the most gorgeous boy she'd ever seen. She double-checked her boarding pass and the seat number. There was no mistake.

"Are you sitting next to *me*?" the boy asked, apparently as pleasantly surprised as Jane.

"That's what it says here," she told him, nodding.

"Well, let me help you with your bag then," he offered, standing up. Gratefully, Jane let him put her bulky coat up in the overhead compartment, and slip her ungainly carry-on bag under her seat. She thanked him as she moved into her seat by the window.

When he sat down, he started reading his magazine again, so Jane buckled herself in and pulled her book out of her bag. She could barely concentrate on the book, wondering when the boy next to her might start up a conversation. Maybe he has a steady girl friend, she thought. Well, then, maybe *she* had a steady boy friend in Cary Slade. But Cary was in Colorado. And then there was Neal in Boston. Wait a minute, she told herself. She wasn't dating this boy who sat next to her. She only wanted to talk to him. Well, he probably lived in Chicago, so there was no way they could see much of each other.

Jane's thinking continued along that line during all of the takeoff preparations. By the time the plane had reached its cruising altitude, she had concluded that it was just as well he lived in Chicago, because they would certainly live in Boston after they were married, and she wouldn't want a lot of bossy in-laws living too close.

She turned another unread page in her book.

"Good book?" he asked.

"I guess so," she said vaguely.

"I figured it had to be or you couldn't possibly be reading it so quickly — unless you took one of those speed-reading course things. Have you?"

"Uh, no." She was getting flustered. Just in time, he changed the subject.

"My name's Zach. Zach Foster."

"I'm Jane Barrett."

"Glad to meet you," he said, twisting awkwardly in his seat and shaking her hand solemnly.

"Same here," she said.

"You coming or going?" he asked her.

"I'm going," she said. "I'm visiting a friend in Chicago. How about you?"

"I'm coming. I live in Chicago. I spent the holiday with my dad near Boston. My parents are divorced, see, so all my vacations are split."

"Oh, I'm sorry," Jane said.

"It's okay. It's been that way since I was a little kid. I'm used to it." Then he changed the subject. "What are you going to do while you're in Chicago?"

"Actually," Jane said, "I'm going to be working. My friend's father owns a restaurant. When it turned out he was going to be short-handed, I offered to come and pitch in."

"Really?"

Jane nodded.

"You've had experience?"

"A little," she told him. His eyes lit up with admiration.

"I think that's great," he said. "You know, so many people our age just never have a chance to learn what work is. Never mind that a lot of times it's not fun, the fact is we'll spend the rest of our lives doing it, so it's really important to begin early."

"Well, I saw this as an opportunity —" Jane began.

"You're right. It *is* an opportunity," he cut in. "You know what I hate?"

"What?"

"I hate people who are rich. Rich people are lazy. They don't *have* to work; so they don't work. Oh, sure, you might find a rich person who would sort of fool around in the working world, but, believe me, Jane, you'll never find a rich person who understands what work is. What it *really* means. You know, blisters on your hands so your family can eat. Know what I mean?"

Jane was stunned. Quickly, she glanced at her manicured hands, imagining blisters. She hid her distaste.

"Of course, I understand, but —" she began, but he cut her off again.

"I know. You've never thought of it that way, have you? You just know that when your friend needed help and you needed a job, the thing to do was to pitch in and do the work. You can make good money earning those tips."

Somehow, Zach's image of who she was and what she was doing just didn't mesh with what was really happening. But it didn't matter, she told herself. He was interesting — and good-looking — and the flight was only an hour and a half. It couldn't matter. She played along.

While Zach continued to speak about the evils of money, Jane tucked her book back into her carry-on bag and pulled out her needlepoint. But as she was threading the needle, she looked down and saw that her expensive cashmere sweater was sticking out of her bag. Surreptitiously, she nudged it back into the bag with her toe. Zach didn't seem to notice.

"Say, maybe we could get together while you're in Chicago, huh?" he asked.

Jane hesitated. She knew *nothing* about him. He was a stranger. But then she decided he was *too* nice.

"That would be fun," she said impulsively. "We'll just be working at night in the restaurant, so I could see you during the day."

"Good idea. Where are you staying?" Zach asked.

"At Andy's house," Jane told him. "Here, I'll give you the address and phone number." She opened her pocketbook and pulled out her address book, hoping Zach wouldn't recognize the designer label etched into the Italian leather. He didn't.

Jotting down the information, he began suggesting outings for them. "How about the Art Institute? Do you like art?"

"Oh, yes, I do," Jane said enthusiastically.

"Boy, Boston was a great place for that.

Have you ever been to the Boston Museum of Fine Arts?"

Jane nodded, thinking of her grandfather's paintings, which hung on the walls there.

"And particularly the Barrett collection — say that's your last name, isn't it? Isn't that a coincidence?"

Jane was too stunned to speak.

"Ladies and gentlemen," the loudspeaker crackled. "We are now entering our final approach to Chicago's O'Hare Airport. Please put your seat backs and tray tables in their full upright and locked position, and extinguish all smoking materials in preparation for our landing."

CHAPTER FIVE

"Jane! Jane! Over here!" Andy yelled.

With a conscious effort, Jane took her eyes from Zach to search the crowd for the familiar voice.

"Hi, Andy!" she called when she spotted her friend. She ran over to her and they hugged warmly. Zach followed her.

"Andy, this is Zach. Zach Foster, meet Andrea Cord. It's her father's restaurant I'll be working at," she explained.

"Glad to meet you, Andy," Zach said, shaking her hand.

"Where's Toby?" Jane asked. "Wasn't her plane due to arrive first?"

"Yes. She's here. She's rounding up her luggage. We'll meet her there. Come on."

Zach and Jane followed Andy down to the luggage claim area. Toby had gotten her duffle bag and was watching to see where Jane's luggage would arrive.

Jane ran and hugged her and then introduced Zach as well.

"Zach and I were seatmates, you see," she told her friends. "And we got to talking and — "

"And Jane was telling me about the job she landed at your father's place for the vacation — "

"Well, it wasn't exactly like that," Andy protested lightly.

"No matter how it happened," Zach said. "She's really lucky to have an opportunity to make some money over the holidays."

"Sure," Andy teased. "She's got to save for college, right?" She and Toby laughed. Jane and Zach didn't. Jane gave her friends a look intended to turn them to stone, so they took the hint and stopped the joke.

"Hey, there's my suitcase," Jane said, relieved to change the subject.

"I'll get that for you," Zach offered, stepping over to the moving luggage carrier.

"I'll explain later," Jane whispered hurriedly to her friends.

Andy and Toby glanced at each other quickly, then realized that Jane had her reasons, so they kept their peace.

"Here you go, Jane," Zach brought her bag over to her. "I'll carry it over to the car for you."

"Thanks, Zach, but I can manage," Jane told him, taking the bag from him.

"Can we give you a lift?" Andy offered. "My

brother Charlie's waiting for us with the car in short-term parking."

"No thanks," he told her. "My mother's going to pick me up here on her way home from work. It'll just be an hour or so."

"Good-bye, Zach," Jane said. "And thanks."

"Thanks for what?" he asked.

"Oh, just thanks for being good company."

"You haven't seen anything yet, Janie," he smiled warmly, gazing into her eyes. "I'm going to be the best tour guide you ever had in Chicago, just you wait and see."

"I'm looking forward to it," she told him, hesitating. *No* one had *ever* called her "Janie" before.

"Just don't get too tired with all that work. We're going to have some fun together."

He was so positive. Everything about him was so positive. Jane had never met another person like that. She was fascinated by him. Zach looked deeply into her eyes. Jane stood frozen by his gaze.

"Come on, Janie!" Andy urged. "We've got to get back to the restaurant before the first diners arrive."

"Right, Andy. 'Bye, Zach."

Jane turned, picked up her bag, and followed her friends out to the parking lot.

"Isn't he gorgeous?" Jane asked her friends as they headed for downtown Chicago.

"Yeah, but this is a little weird, Jane," Toby began.

"No need to worry about our *Janie*, Toby," Andy began, using Zach's version of Jane's name. "Within an hour, she's going to be so busy at Dad's restaurant that she won't have time to think about her Sir Galahad. She'll be concentrating on the money she's earning toward her college education!"

They giggled and Jane had to join them. The idea really was funny.

"Oh, I know, he got all the wrong ideas about me, but he was so positive he knew what he was talking about, I just didn't have the heart to correct him. What does it matter, anyway? It was just a little bit of fun, right?"

"Sure, Janie. I just hope it stays that way," Andy said, ominously. But Jane didn't see what there was to worry about.

"And speaking of boyfriends," Jane continued. "Two days ago, I had a call from Cornelius Worthington One-Two-Three. He was just absolutely all full of questions about you, Toby. I think Neal's considering abandoning his affection for Boston Brahmin Society and becoming a genuine cowpoke. At the same time he was getting so angry with me for the mix-up at Alison's wedding, he was apparently developing a crush on you."

"Me?" was all Toby could say.

"I think so," Jane said. "You *are* the 'sweet redhead from Texas' he mentioned, aren't you?"

"Well, I, uh, just don't know what made him say, or think, or I mean — " Toby couldn't go on. She didn't have to. Her bright red cheeks revealed both her embarrassment and her pleasure at the compliment from Neal.

"Ain't love grand?" Jane asked. Her friends nodded in agreement.

An hour later, Jane and Toby were getting their final instructions as professional waitresses.

"Sure, you've eaten in hundreds of restaurants, but there's a lot that goes on that you're never aware of at all."

"Like what?" Jane asked.

"Like you always notice when your waiter or waitress isn't available the second you want to order something. But you *never* notice the times that he or she magically appears at just the right moment."

"How does that happen?" Jane asked.

"It happens because the server is constantly on the lookout for signs of need. For instance, diners get their menus as soon as they arrive and the bartender takes any drink orders then. Usually, people don't look at the menus right away, but the good server notices when they *do* start looking at their menus, and as soon as all the menus are lowered to the table, you know people are ready to order. That's your magic cue."

"I never really thought about it," Jane said.

"Me, neither," Toby agreed. "But it makes sense."

"Oh, it all makes sense," Andy assured them. "And it's easy enough to do, too. Particularly if you're the kind of person who can keep eight things at a time straight in your mind."

"You mean, like who's dawdling over the salad bar, and who wants theirs medium, and which party said they had to hurry to get to a show on time?" Toby asked.

"Right, just like that," Andy nodded. "Okay, now to uniforms."

"Uniforms?" Jane asked, recalling how thoroughly she'd planned her wardrobe.

"Sure, we all dress the same, and here they are." Jane opened the closet in the locker room to reveal a rack full of clean uniforms.

"Hey, swell," Toby said. "These are much nicer than the little pink things the waitresses had to wear in the diner."

"Didn't you wear one, too?" Andy asked.

"Oh, *no*," Toby said.

"Then you *weren't* a waitress?" Andy asked suspiciously.

"Oh. Well," Toby confessed cheerfully, "I took care of the horses. It was a sort of diner/stable combination place."

"I thought you — " Andy tried to speak.

"Well, I *did* work there," Toby said earnestly.

"I suppose so, but just don't give any of our customers any oats, okay?" Andy said.

"Okay," Toby agreed.

"Good, now let's try on the uniforms. They

usually look all right on the waitresses."

Jane decided to keep her opinion to herself. It wasn't likely to do her much good to express it, and it certainly wasn't going to make anybody else change their minds. Smiling bravely, she reached for one that looked sort of like her size.

Within a few minutes, they were all dressed identically. It wasn't so bad after all. They wore navy blue skirts and light blue blouses. There were small white aprons which tied around their waists and blue and white caps. At Andy's suggestion, Toby and Jane had brought the most comfortable shoes they had. Toby had resisted the temptation to bring her riding boots. They each wore running shoes.

"Not bad," Andy remarked, admiring the trio in the mirror. "Not bad at all. In fact, I think we look like a bunch of old pros."

Jane and Toby weren't so sure.

"Greenhorns," Toby corrected her. "Real tenderfoots."

"Not for long," Andy told her. "What do you think, Jane?"

"Well, it's not so bad, Andy. In fact, I think that if I use that really neat blue hair spray you gave me for Christmas, why, it would be a perfect match!"

"Try it, just try it!" Andy challenged and they all laughed. "Okay, now, team, here are your weapons."

Andy handed each of them an order pad on the back of which had been taped tonight's specials. Each got two pens. "Someone will take your pen. They won't mean to. But when they pay with credit cards, a lot of the time they take the pen."

Jane and Toby were amused to find that their aprons had special slots for pens and a pocket that was just the right size for the order pad.

"Neat," Toby remarked.

"Ready?" Andy asked.

"Ready!" Toby and Jane answered in a single triumphant voice.

"Then let's get to work," Andy said firmly. "We start with the grand tour."

"The Cook's Tour?" Jane punned.

"No, actually, the cook's *daughter's* tour," Andy corrected her, leading the way.

CHAPTER SIX

Steak 'n Ribs was on three floors. In the basement were the food storage rooms and the staff dressing room. The main floor had the kitchen and the main dining room. The top floor was the banquet room.

"First stop: the basement. Except for the dressing room, which you've already seen, you won't spend much time here," Andy told her friends. "But it's really important, because this is where all the stuff that's not being used is stored."

"Like food?" Toby asked.

"Sure, the food, but also extra tables, chairs, linen — stuff like that. As soon as the holidays are over, all the Christmas things will be down here. We stow the artificial tree over in that corner." She pointed to a small niche. "When I was a little girl, every time I wanted it to be Christmas, I'd just come down here and plug the thing in."

Jane and Toby smiled at this glimpse into their friend's past.

"One thing I must warn you about. When the restaurant is open, we keep this whole area locked. Too many customers think this is the way to the rest rooms and the stairs are dark and steep. The last thing we need is to have some customer stumbling down them in the dark."

That made sense. Andy showed them where the key was kept and explained how to work the lock. "Next stop, the kitchen," Andy told them, locking the door behind her and leading the way.

The kitchen was a large room, edged by stoves and stainless-steel refrigerators. It was divided along the center by steam tables at the assembly area. The idea was that the food was cooked at the stoves and transferred to the steam tables, where it was kept warm until assembled.

When the orders came in to the assembly area, the First Cook would make up the plates and, when the order was complete, put the assembled tray under the warming lights by the kitchen entrance. At that time, the First Cook would ring the particular waiter or waitress's signal. The waitress could pick up the completed order and deliver it to the happy diners.

"Why is the person who assembles the plates called the First *Cook*?" Toby asked.

"I used to wonder the same thing myself," Andy confessed. "Then I decided it was that first he — or she — *cooks*, then assembles."

Jane and Toby gave her a withering look, then they all laughed.

"And at this end," Andy led them to the far side of the kitchen, "is the Cook's Table. That's the name for the place where the staff eats. That's us. We're staff." The Cook's Table was a large rectangular table with ten chairs around it. "Also, if you're taking a break, you can come in here and rest. It's not a good idea to sit down where diners can see you."

"You don't want them to see our total exhaustion?" Toby asked brightly.

"Oh, it's not that," Andy told her. "It's just that if a customer sees you sitting down, he'll think of something he needs. Bye-bye break time! Now come see where you'll spend most of your time." Andy led them through the swinging doors of the kitchen to the main room on the first floor.

The dining room was wood-paneled, giving it a country-comfort look, informal but welcoming. All the tables were covered with blue tablecloths, matching the girls' skirts, and light blue napkins, matching their blouses. The chairs were wooden, with blue-cushioned seats. On cold winter nights, such as this one, a cozy fire blazed in the big brick fireplace that occupied most of the back wall of the room. The effect was pleasant and friendly.

Upstairs was the banquet room, a carbon

copy of the dining room, but larger, since there was no kitchen on that floor. All the food was transferred to the banquets by two large dumbwaiters, "For food only," Andy warned them before she led her friends back downstairs.

She took them back to the Cook's Table where they got a fast bite to eat and some final instructions on the fine art of waitressing from Andy. When Toby and Jane had swallowed as much as they could of each, they reported to work in the dining room.

"Hurry, girls," Andy's dad, Mike Cord, told them. "We've already got two groups in the restaurant, and a third is taking off their coats now. Tonight, I want you girls to work the main floor. There's a wedding reception in the party room upstairs, and the others can take care of that. Andy, you cover Section A; that's tables 16 through 21 in the corner. Jane, you get B; that's tables 10 through 15. Toby, you're on C, Tables 6 through 10. Steve's on Section D, 1 through 5. Charlie and Ted will cover the party room. Andy and Jane, get to work. Toby, the next party in is yours."

That was it. After that, they were all working, all night long. Jane and Toby watched as Andy approached the group of diners at Table 18.

"Good evening," she said politely. "My name is Andy, and I'd be pleased to take your order when you're ready."

"Oh, we're in no rush, Andy, thank you,"

one woman told her. "We're going to have something to drink and then we'll order."

"Would you like to hear the specials now?" Andy asked.

"In a few minutes," they told her.

"Fine, I'll be back," she assured them.

At her table, Jane tried to follow suit.

"Hi, I'm Jane," she said. "Would you like to order now?"

"Yes," one of the men said. "Right away, please. We have an eight o'clock show and we don't want to be late."

"Okay, let me tell you the specials." Jane was pleased at how official she sounded.

"I don't want any of the specials," one of the women said. "I want to have the same thing I had when I came last time."

"Certainly, what was that?" Jane asked.

"I'm not sure, but it was a veal dish. There was sort of a brown sauce, I think it may have been a white wine sauce. No, I guess it was red. It was delicious."

"I'm afraid I don't know what that was, but I'll ask the chef. Would the others like to order now?"

"No, I want to hear the specials — "

"Okay, fine," Jane said, flipping her order pad. "Tonight's specials are — " she paled as she looked at the pad. The first item on it was: "gr. lb. ch. w/ g Ps+ prsly. n. pot. $8.95."

"I have no idea what the specials are tonight," she told the people frankly. "Why don't you all have that wonderful dish the lady enjoyed last time she was here?"

Stunned, the diners agreed. Jane scurried off to the kitchen to find out what it was.

Fortunately, Ina Cord, Andy's mother, knew exactly what the lady was trying to describe and had enough servings for the table, although that special was not on the menu that night. Jane beamed proudly at her first success while she served her guests. In the meantime, however, she had cornered Andy for a translation of the specials.

"That's easy, Jane," Andy assured her. "It means grilled lamb chops, served with green peas and new potatoes with parsley for $8.95."

"Easy," Jane remarked sarcastically. "I was going to tell them it was a pound of green cheese with great possibilities — and it went downhill from there!"

Swiftly, Andy translated the rest of the specials for Jane, and Jane vowed to read them over and practice them when she had a minute. But she didn't have a minute now.

"Miss!" came the loud cry. Everyone in the restaurant turned to the man who'd yelled. "You, Miss! With the red hair." It was the group of people Toby was serving. Toby hurried over to the table.

"Yes, sir, what can I do for you?"

"This steak was supposed to be medium, not rare!" he said rudely.

"I'll take care of that, sir," she assured him,

whisking his plate away and taking it back to the kitchen for more cooking.

Jane was too busy watching Toby handle the sticky situation perfectly to hear the insistent chime *dee-dee-da*. She watched while Mr. Cord led the wedding reception guests upstairs to the party room. *Dee-dee-da*. She watched the bartender mix drinks for eight people, place them expertly on the tray and serve them without having to ask who had ordered what. *Dee-dee-da*.

"Jane, that's you!" Andy hissed.

"Me?"

"Your signal. Remember, dee-dee-da? Your order's ready."

"Oh, my goodness. I forgot." Embarrassed, she hurried over to the assembly area. There, six plates awaited her, cooling rapidly. She put them onto a tray and carried it over to the table while the busboy opened the tray rack for her. She set the tray down and began serving. She'd forgotten to put the plates in order and she'd left the order pad by the assembly area.

"Who gets the chicken?" she asked.

"I do," said one lady. Jane put the plate in front of her.

"No *I* ordered that," her husband said.

"You're right. Mine is the *fried* chicken. So you get that."

"But this one has mushrooms on the side and I hate mushrooms. Can you have them removed? I thought I was getting yellow beans with it," the husband said with annoyance.

"Oh, then maybe yours is this chicken with red stuff on it and yellow beans on the side?" Jane suggested.

"Red stuff?" the woman said. "Perhaps you mean tomato sauce?"

"Yes, Ma'am," Jane said, flustered and barely controlling her fury.

Eventually, Jane got all the orders straightened out but she vowed never to forget to put the plates in serving order again. She didn't want any more discussions about red stuff and mushrooms.

Just as she was returning to the kitchen, her eye caught a look from one of her other tables. In a glance, it told her that she'd been forgetting about the cream to go with the coffee that she'd served ten minutes before. She rushed to the condiment station and carried the cream and sugar to the guests, along with her apologies.

"I'm *really* sorry," she told them. "I'm actually new at this and I'm trying, but there's so much to learn."

"Yes," the man said coolly. "We know you have a lot to learn. We've been coming here a long time, and the service is usually very good. Maybe it's just the busy season."

"Maybe," Jane said. "Thanks for being understanding." She left them with their coffee, relieved to have gotten off the hook once again. Jane was getting a new understanding and appreciation of waitresses.

"Jane!" Toby hissed.

"What did I forget now?"

"Nothing, but I need some help."

"With what?"

"I can't get this calculator to work and these people are waiting for their bill. You're a whiz at math. Can you do it? My chime's been going crazy, too. I've got to serve those six hungry diners in the corner — "

"Sure, Toby. I've got a break for a second. I'll tote it for you."

Jane took the bill over to the calculator and began the math. It wasn't complicated, but Toby was obviously flustered. It was easy enough to see how that could happen. Jane concentrated on the figures. It seemed so coolly logical after the confusion of taking orders and serving. When she was done, she turned around to look for Toby and give her the bill.

What she saw, however, was something else. Toby held the tray proudly with one hand above her shoulder, balancing it with the other. One of the diners at another table stood up. He was backing away from his table, finishing telling a story as he backed off. It would have been all right, but it was a fishing story.

". . . and to this day, he claims that trout was *this* big!" The man said, as he spread his arms to demonstrate.

His left arm caught Toby in the stomach. The uplifted tray tilted forward. The man turned and stumbled, grabbing Toby's right arm for support.

It didn't work.

First the man fell down. Then Toby lost her balance and fell down next to him. Finally, the six delicious meals slid off the toppling tray, crashing onto the restaurant's floor with a thunderous clanging.

And then there was silence.

CHAPTER SEVEN

I don't believe this," Andy said, slipping into her pajamas and climbing under the covers in a single smooth motion. "I'm too tired to talk. All I could think of last week was how much fun we'd have swapping stories nightly, but" — she interrupted herself with a yawn — "tonight, that's the last thing I want to do."

"Shhh," Jane said quietly. "Toby's asleep already."

"I'm not," Toby protested weakly. "But I will be in just a minute. . . ." Her voice trailed off, replaced by deep, even breathing. In seconds Jane and Andy were asleep, too.

"Jane, dear," Mrs. Cord's pleasant voice awoke her. "Jane, there's a phone call for you. Someone named Zach?"

"I'm sorry, his order isn't ready yet," Jane responded, obviously deep in a dream. "If he's really hungry, he should go back to the salad bar." She rolled over.

"No, Jane," Ina Cord said patiently. "Wake up, dear. This is not the restaurant. You've got a phone call from some boy named Zach. Do you want me to have him call you back?"

Jane's eyes sprang open. "Zach?"

Then she remembered — the gorgeous boy on the airplane. It was only yesterday, but it seemed so long ago. She glanced at her watch. Ten-thirty. She'd just slept ten hours. How could she be so tired?

"Right, Zach. I'll take it," she said, and stood up with determination. She walked sleepily out of the room to the telephone in the kitchen.

"Hi, Zach."

"Good morning, sleepy-head," he greeted her.

"It's not 'good,' Zach," she told him. "I'm exhausted. And my feet ache — "

"Too much to go to the Art Institute with me this afternoon?"

"Well, maybe they don't ache *that* much," Jane admitted.

"Good, then I'll pick you up at the Cords' at noon. We can have lunch in the cafeteria at the museum. I'll have you back in time to serve dinner. Sound okay?"

"Sounds great, Zach." Except for the part about serving dinner, she thought to herself. "See you then," she said to Zach.

" 'Bye, Jane."

" 'Bye."

Jane turned and faced Mrs. Cord sheepishly. "That was Zach. I met him on the plane."

Mrs. Cord raised her eyebrows. "And you're going out with him?"

"I can tell he's a very nice boy, Mrs. Cord," Jane said.

Ina Cord poured three glasses of orange juice. "We'll see. When he gets here I want to meet him. I want to know his parents' names, his address, and his phone number. Then we'll see."

Jane nodded and rubbed her eyes.

"Here you go, Jane," Ina Cord said, handing her a glass of orange juice. "You can take some in for the other two sleepy-heads, too."

Gratefully, Jane downed the orange juice. Then she carried two full glasses back to her friends.

"Wake-up time!" she said, as cheerfully as she could, handing out the orange juice. "Would you like to hear the specials?"

"What service!" Toby remarked.

"And tea follows," Jane promised. "If you get it yourselves! I'm off waitressing until 5:30 tonight."

"Just what do you plan to do in the meantime?" Andy asked suspiciously.

"I've got a date with Zach. *If* you're mother approves of him. He's picking me up in — " she glanced at her watch again. "Oh, my goodness! It's just an hour and fifteen minutes.

I've got to do my hair, my nails. I need to press my silk blouse. How can I get that all done?"

"Boy, you really want to impress this guy, don't you?" Toby asked. Jane nodded. Toby continued. "But he didn't seem to me like the kind that's going to be impressed with polished nails and silk blouses."

Jane was brought up short. "Yes, of course, you're right. This is going to take some thinking."

"Well, Toby," Andy began. "While she's thinking, tell me how *you* are this morning."

"I guess I'm alive," she said hesitantly. "But to tell the truth, I feel like I spent most of yesterday breaking in broncos. My arms and shoulders hurt from carrying trays. My fingers hurt from writing quickly. My ribs hurt from where the tray hit me when that man landed on me. My feet hurt from a million miles of walking between the kitchen and the tables."

"That all?" Andy asked.

"Nope. To tell the truth, my pride's a little bruised, too."

"Why?" Andy queried.

"I never made so many silly mistakes doing anything in my whole life," Toby confessed.

"I thought you did wonderfully," Andy reassured her. "I told you, waitressing is hard work, but you learned from everything you did, and once we got you cleaned up from the disaster, everything went smoothly. You were *great*."

"Me, too?" Jane asked.

"You, too," Andy said.

"Really?"

"Of course, really. And tonight's going to be better."

"In what way?" Toby asked.

"Well, you've both already made all the really dumb mistakes new waitresses make, so you won't make them again!"

"That's the nicest thing I've heard all day," Toby said, laughing wryly.

"Not me," said Jane. "The best news I've had today is from Zach."

"Sure," said Andy. "But what are you going to wear?"

Jane didn't know. She'd surveyed her traveling wardrobe, and none of it seemed right for Zach. "Somehow, nothing I own seems right to go out with Zach."

"Maybe you'd better ease on down to Marshall Field's," Andy teased. Jane wasn't in a teasing mood, however.

"I don't think that's right, either," she said.

"How about the Army/Navy Surplus store on the corner?" Toby suggested.

"Hmmm," Jane pondered. "Say, Andy, can I borrow your jeans?"

"Sure."

"And Toby, did you bring that green sweatshirt?"

"Yeah, you want to borrow that, too?"

"If I may," Jane said.

"Sure," Toby agreed. "But it's really kind

of scuzzy. I usually wear it riding, but it's been washed, so it doesn't smell of horses."

"Thanks. Then I can wear my silk turtleneck under the sweat shirt and the designer initials won't show."

"Want me to remove the 'Levi's' label from the jeans?" Andy offered jokingly.

The humor went right past Jane. "No, I don't think so," she said. "Levi's aren't really designer jeans, see. So it doesn't matter."

"Good idea, Jane," Andy told her with a little ice in her voice. "You can borrow poor people's clothes from Toby and me, and nobody will ever know you're an heiress."

"Oh, it's not that," Jane told her friends. "I just don't want Zach to be uncomfortable."

Even Toby was startled by this. "Zach, uncomfortable? How about you?"

Jane didn't seem to understand what her friend was asking. "Oh, no. I won't be uncomfortable. Andy and I are just about the same size — and the sweat shirt's supposed to be baggy."

Andy and Toby exchanged glances, but before they could say anything to Jane — as if she would have understood them — she bounded off to the shower, filled with excitement about her upcoming date.

"You look great," Zach told Jane as they walked out of Andy's apartment, after he had passed Mrs. Cord's careful scrutiny. "And it's a good thing you've dressed warmly. There's nothing like a Chicago winter day — unless it's a Chicago winter evening!"

Jane was still unprepared for the blast of cold wind which greeted her in front of Andy's building. Boston could be cold, but nothing like this!

"Come on, Jane, put on the hat," Zach coaxed her.

"But it looks so silly," she protested.

"It looks a lot better than frostbitten ears."

Jane slipped the triple-thick woolen hat over her head. Within a very few seconds, she was awfully glad she had it.

"We just have a six-block walk to the bus," Zach said. "That bus will take us right along Michigan Avenue to the Art Institute."

"Okay, mush!" Jane said, welcoming Zach's warm arm across her shoulders. A little bit of her wondered what his reaction would be if she offered to pay for a cab. She decided not to try to find out.

The Art Institute was everything Jane had thought it would be. She'd always heard about their collection of American Modernists, but her favorite part was the Impressionist collection.

"I like these best, too," Zach agreed. "The Barrett Collection at the Museum of Fine Arts in Boston is great, but these, well maybe I just know them best."

Jane studied a Monet painting for a while. Monet's depiction of color and light just fascinated her. Also, she needed to concentrate on something so she wouldn't give Zach an argument about the Barrett Collection. That seemed like pretty thin ice to her.

"You know, they've got a school of fine arts in the museum here?"

"Yes, I know," she said. Of course she knew: Her mother was on its Board of Trustees.

"I'm thinking of attending it. I'm pretty sure I want to be an artist. I don't know if I'll be able to get in, though. You really need someone to sponsor you, and that's pretty hard to do. I don't think my art teacher has much sway with the admissions committee."

Suddenly, Jane was annoyed. She knew that one word from her mother would get Zach into this art school — or any other. But she couldn't let him know about that, or he wouldn't be her friend. It seemed ironic to her that she'd lose his friendship if she tried to do the very thing he most wanted. She almost took the chance, but then Zach spoke.

"I don't know why I even think about it," he said. "The Board of Trustees is made up of rich snobs, and so the school is pretty much the same thing. I'm just going to forget about it."

Jane was relieved. Zach had quite an ability to confuse her. He managed to make everything she took for granted seem topsy-turvy. She remembered making fun of her mother's fund-raising teas and all the boring old ladies her mother had to be nice to. Was it really any different for her to make fun of the rich old ladies and for Zach to do it? Somehow, it felt like it was. But, she told herself, it couldn't be.

Zach slipped his arm through hers while she gazed at the painting. "Come on, Jane. Let's have lunch in the cafeteria."

"Great idea!" she answered. "I'll have a chance to see how another kind of restaurant works."

"And to rest your feet — "

"I didn't want to say anything about that," Jane admitted.

"I know you didn't. You're a real fighter, Jane. I admire that."

Jane smiled warmly at Zach. He was easy to smile at. His deep brown eyes sparkled just looking at her.

How could anything be wrong when she felt so happy?

For a brief moment, she thought of Cary. But she wasn't doing anything *wrong*. How could looking at paintings in the Chicago Art Institute be wrong!

CHAPTER EIGHT

O kay, now here are some tips on how to make this job easier."

Jane and Toby listened attentively to Andy. Anything they could do to make it easier would be great.

"One of the things you want to do is to limit the number of trips you make to the kitchen. So, everytime you're heading back, look around for something to carry with you."

"That makes it *easier*?" Jane asked dubiously.

"Sure does," a deep male voice interrupted.

The three girls turned to see Steve Palmer. Steve lived a few blocks away from the Cords, and helped in the restaurant when he was needed. He paused on his way to his locker.

"You see," he explained. "You're going to have to pick up all the dishes on the tables at some time, so you might as well do it while you're going back to the kitchen anyway."

That made some sense. "Listen to Andy," he told Jane and Toby. "She knows what she's talking about. She's terrific."

Almost as if to punctuate the thought, Steve strode through the kitchen door, which swung open silently and closed with a breathy "hppph!" He was gone.

"Well, I guess we've been told!" Toby teased.

"It isn't every waitress who gets to train with a *superstar*," Jane joined in.

"Oh, come on, girls," Andy said, clearly embarrassed.

"Quit the humility act with us, Andy. We know greatness. We're in awe." Looking at Andy, Jane realized that she wasn't finding it funny, so she stopped talking.

"I don't know why he said that," Andy said.

"You don't?" Toby asked, surprised.

"No, I don't."

"Andy, dear, use those beautiful brown eyes and that razor-sharp intellect of yours," Jane suggested.

"Still doesn't make sense to me," Andy said.

"It's because he's crazy about you," Toby informed her.

"But he's in college," Andy protested.

"So?" her friends responded together.

"But he's so good-looking," Andy said.

"And you're not?" Jane asked.

"But he's so *nice*."

"The same could be said for you," Jane retorted.

"But he never even speaks to me unless it's to ask where the relish tray is — or the dessert menus. Or, uh, last week, he asked me about the pot-pie special."

"Some romance!" Toby said, disappointed.

"See what I mean? It's all business with him. Relish trays and pot-pie specials do not a long-term relationship make," Andy said. "I've always wanted him to notice me, but he never does."

Jane nodded wisely. "I've got to admit it, Andy. He looks like a perfect match for you, but if, after ten days, you still haven't gotten beyond dessert menus, the future is bleak."

"Not everybody gets taken to the Art Institute on their first date," Toby reminded her friends. Jane smiled in recollection.

"Yeah, and we're going out again tonight, too."

"Tonight?" Andy said in disbelief.

"Sure, Zach is picking me up here after the kitchen closes. He said I really needed to be outdoors in a Chicago winter night to know what cold means."

"And then he'll show you what warm is?" Andy challenged her.

"I think there's an all-night diner near here. He said they're famous for their hot chocolate. We won't be long. I'll be too tired to stay out late, anyway."

"Judging from last night," Andy told her, "you'll be too tired to *go* out late."

"I can take care of myself," Jane said, a bit too harshly.

"I'm sure you can, Jane. I'm sorry if I sounded bossy. I'm just concerned," Andy said.

"Thanks, Andy. I'll get enough sleep, though."

Andy realized that nothing she could say was going to have any useful effect on Jane. She changed the subject.

"Now, look. Here's how we can work in teams so that we should end up doing less backing and forthing. Steve and I were doing this last week, and it worked pretty well."

Andy then explained how they could save their feet.

At Andy's request, Steve teamed with Toby to help her and improve her skills. Andy teamed with Jane for instruction. Jane was trying very hard, and most of the time she was successful. Still, Andy found that she had very little patience with Jane.

"Water for Table 21," Andy snapped.

"I did it already," Jane told her.

"Well, I see a glass that's gotten way down."

"So fill it," Jane said. Somehow, teaming with Andy tonight had gotten to mean that Andy gave orders and Jane followed them. Jane shrugged and watched Andy fill the glass.

At least she was learning how to cope with the great demands of the job.

Jane spotted one of her tables where the diners were just putting down their forks. She walked over to it.

"May I clear?" she asked politely.

"Yes, thank you." They smiled at her.

See, she said to herself, there's nothing to this. You just keep absolutely everything in mind, and it works perfectly.

Andy joined her, helping to clear, picking up the dishes before Jane could get to them. "Table 17 is ready to order," she whispered, her voice tinged with annoyance.

Jane decided not to let it get to her.

"Can do," she said, promising herself to hold her temper until they could talk in private. She went over to the table and pulled out her order pad. She stood there expectantly. The diners looked at her in confusion.

"Ready to order?" she asked politely

"We just *did* order," one of them said. "Didn't you tell the chef yet? Remember that I want that steak *well*-done."

"I'm sorry," Jane said, stepping away. How could she have forgotten that group, she wondered. Each person had had very specific requests about how their meat should be done. Jane had wished she'd had color swatches for them to choose from. She couldn't wait for the inevitable complaints.

Jane flipped to the map of the room. It was Table 18 that had given her such trouble.

She turned to Table 17 behind her. "Ready to order?" she asked.

"No, not yet," the man said. Jane could tell that they wanted to dawdle over their drinks before ordering. Okay, that gave her a break.

Andy was done clearing the other table, and everything else was in process. For a few minutes, there was nothing to do. Jane slipped into the kitchen and found an unoccupied stool at the Cook's Table.

When Andy came into the kitchen, too, Jane waved an invitation to her. She came and sat down beside her.

"I'm sorry if I'm klutzy sometimes, Andy," Jane began.

"I suppose you can't help it," Andy said ungraciously.

"I'm *trying* to help it!" Jane countered, annoyed. She had hoped her opening would forestall cross words. Apparently she was wrong. "Look, Andy, I don't want to argue with you. I know you like a guy who won't notice you. And now I'm going out with Zach tonight."

"You think I'm annoyed with you because I'm jealous?" Andy asked, astonished.

"Well, sure," Jane said. "It's natural."

"Just like pretending to be something you're not is natural?"

"What are you talking about?" Jane asked. "I'm not *pretending* to be a waitress. I'm trying to *be* a waitress."

Andy could tell from the tone of Jane's

voice that Jane absolutely didn't know what she meant.

"Come on, let's add our bills now," Andy suggested, changing the subject. They each pulled out their pads and began correcting and adding.

Jane glanced at her watch. It was 10:10. Twenty minutes until last orders. Forty-five minutes after that, Zach would arrive. The crowd was already thinning out. It was less hectic. She and Toby stood near the kitchen door, watching diners, waiting for a signal.

"Jane and Toby!" Mike Cord called. They went over to him.

"It's getting quiet down here, but things are building up at the banquet upstairs. In about five minutes the dessert soufflés are going to be ready. They have to be served immediately; otherwise they turn into pancakes — tough pancakes. But the tables upstairs aren't cleared yet. You two go on upstairs and help Ted and Charlie until 10:30. Andy and Steve can cover the main floor."

Jane and Toby nodded, handing over their order pads to Mr. Cord. They hurried upstairs to the banquet room.

"Dessert's up for 22," Andy told Steve. He nodded and swept the plates onto a tray to serve them while Andy cleared 23, taking coffee and dessert orders and providing the necessary doggie bag for the uneaten steak.

"I'll clear 17, you take 13's order," Steve suggested while he passed Andy carrying 22's dessert. Andy nodded, heading for 13. By the time she had 13's order, 17's dessert was ready. And so it went. She and Steve were working at almost breakneck speed, the two of them covering more than fifteen occupied tables, but they seemed to be able to work together like a well-choreographed ballet.

"Seconds on coffee for 17."

"Eighteen'll want some, too."

"I'll tote up for 22 — "

"They ordered an additional cheese cake."

"Got it."

"Good."

And it was good. Andy really enjoyed working with Steve. While she stood in place and added up bills for a few minutes, she kept glancing at Steve, working quickly, efficiently, but almost effortlessly. It was a pleasure to see him do his job.

But he was all business with her — no pleasure.

"Tote 17 and 18," he said in thanks for the bill for 22. She nodded, glad to be finishing the bills. That meant the evening was almost over.

And Jane would be going out with Zach.

Andy thought about it for a minute. Maybe she *was* jealous. After all, she'd like nothing better than to know she'd be going out with Steve after work.

No, that wasn't the reason she was an-

noyed with Jane, and it didn't have anything
to do with Cary Slade, either. Jane and Cary
had been dating all term, but Jane was free
to date someone else. Andy was just annoyed
that Jane was lying to Zach. She wondered
how Jane could like someone she had to lie to
so he would be interested in her. Well, Jane
could be pretty stubborn at times, and this was
one of them.

"Close out Table 21," Steve said, giving
Andy their final order.

"Then all that's left is Table 4 and Table
7."

"Right, and the good news is that 7 is full
of dieters, and they won't want your mom's
delicious desserts."

Andy turned to smile at Steve, but he was
already gone, ready to clear Table 4, but not
to rush them. When he came back again for
Table 21's bill, Andy was ready.

"Here you go, Steve. Say, we're just about
done, want to have a soda and dessert in the
kitchen when we close out?"

"No thanks, Andy," he said, it seemed almost too quickly. "I've go to be getting home
soon."

Sure, Andy thought, wistfully. Maybe he's
got an aging mother he takes care of. Or maybe he's got a girl friend he's meeting later.
They'll go out for a Coke. . . .

Andy concentrated on her addition. So
hard that she broke her pencil.

CHAPTER NINE

G ood-night," Mike Cord said warmly.

"Good-night," the man returned. "And thank you."

"Oh, thank *you*."

"You're welcome. Good-night." The party shuffled out the door, into the cold night in search of taxicabs.

Mr. Cord shut the door, flipped the sign from OPEN to CLOSED, and flicked off the neon light.

"That's the sweetest sound in the world, you know," Mrs. Cord said.

"Sure is," agreed Andy.

"Huh?" said Toby.

"The sound of that light being turned off," Andy explained. "It means the night's over. The midnight clean-up crew can come in, and we can go home."

"You're right, then. That *is* the sweetest sound," Toby concurred.

74

"Next to the ringing of the cash register," Mr. Cord corrected her.

They all laughed.

"Come on," Ina Cord invited them. "Time for cake and milk in the kitchen. During a quiet time today, I experimented with a new chocolate recipe. I didn't put it on the menu because I wanted to try it out on family first."

"Sort of like the royal tasters?" Jane teased.

"Don't worry, Jane," Andy assured her. "I'll be a guinea pig for Mom's cakes any day at all. I actually decided to go into ballet years ago in self-defense against my mother's cooking. Without the vigorous exercise of ballet, I'd be blimp-shaped!"

"Enough talk! Let's pour the milk and get down to serious business," Andy's brother, Charlie, interrupted.

Without further ado, they gathered around the chef's table in the kitchen and the cake was served. In spite of being very tired, Jane was pleasantly relaxed at the table. She really loved being among Andy's family. There was a loving warmth that surrounded them and that was readily shared with friends. It was no surprise that the family restaurant was successful. Everyone who came to eat there was made to feel like part of the family — just like everyone who worked there.

"So who's coming to family lunch tomorrow?"

"Family lunch?" Toby echoed in question.

"Oh, I forgot to tell you about that, huh?" Andy said.

"Yeah, you were too busy telling us about serving from the left and clearing from the right — " Toby began.

"And spilling trays," Jane said. Then she and Toby exchanged looks and laughed. "Some teacher you are," Jane chided her.

"It's not work," Andy assured her quickly. "It's a tradition. Well, I guess it is work, but it's fun work. I mean, the restaurant is closed, but we have a lunch party for family and friends every Wednesday. It's a big buffet, with all kinds of leftovers, and great dishes the chef is experimenting with."

"If all the experiments are as successful as this cake, then there's nothing to worry about," Toby said.

"There's nothing to worry about," Andy's brother, Ted, assured her.

"Anyway," Andy continued, "everyone's welcome. It's sort of an open house."

Jane realized that this might be an opportunity to introduce her friends to Zach. "Could I invite Zach?" Jane asked Ina Cord.

"Of course, dear. He'd be very welcome."

Just then, as if on cue, there was a tap at the front window. "There he is now," Jane said. "I'll see you in a while. I won't be late."

"Doesn't matter to us," Toby assured her. "We won't wait up anyway!" Jane left the room, and the restaurant, to the squeal of laughter behind her.

* * *

Jane slipped out into the freezing darkness where Zach waited for her.

"Zach?"

"Hi, Jane," he greeted her warmly. "Tired?"

"Well, it was pretty rough tonight, but I'm okay. I think I'm getting used to it."

He put his arm around her shoulders and then they began to walk.

"Feet hurt?" he asked.

"No, it's not really my feet. It's more, oh, I don't know. Sort of all over exhaustion. I mean, this is very hard work."

"Are they overworking you?" he asked protectively.

Suddenly his concern was overwhelming to Jane. She simply couldn't resist the sympathy. She knew perfectly well that she wasn't working any harder than anybody else, and she knew that she wasn't any more tired than anybody else, but it seemed so nice to have somebody want to comfort her.

"Let's just say, I'm doing my best, but — " she shrugged.

"Janie, your best is the most that anybody can ask for, so if that's not good enough for them — "

"It's not that, Zach. It's just that, well, it's hard work."

"So here's a place to rest your feet," Zach told her, opening the door to the all-night diner he'd promised. They entered and went to a booth in the back. Zach ordered cocoa for both of them. Chocolate reminded Jane of the family lunch.

"Say, I've got an invitation for you," she said, removing her mittens.

"Me?"

"Yes, you. Will you join us — that is the Cords — for lunch tomorrow at the restaurant?" She took off her warm hat and shook out her long blond hair, running her fingers through the tangles.

"Well sure," he said, pleased. Jane explained the tradition and the kind of party it was. Zach was very happy to be included in the family, even though he didn't know them.

"Knowing the Cords is like falling off a log. They are the *nicest* people, Zach. It's almost impossible to believe. I mean, one day you've never met them and the next day, you're part of the family. I suppose I should have been prepared — from the way Andy is, I mean — but I've really never seen anything like that group."

"Even though they're working you so hard?"

"That has nothing to do with it. You'll see what I mean."

"Yeah, that'll be great. Thanks. Now, tell me all the exciting things that went on tonight in the world of elegant dining."

Their hot chocolate, topped with mounds of whipped cream and shaved bits of chocolate arrived.

"Let me see," Jane mused. "Okay, well first there was the family of six, all of whom ordered steak, and all of whom wanted it done in different ways. The mother just sat there, looking benignly happy while they snapped out orders." Jane pursed her lips and batted her eyes in imitation of one of the fussy customers. " 'I want mine medium-rare, but you know, not so much rare as medium, like he wants his more rare than medium. And *my* baked potato should have chives, but not sour cream, like hers, but with extra butter.' " Zach laughed at her imitation. "It was something. No wonder the mother was so happy to not have to cook for that group!"

"Boy, when I was a kid, we would have been happy to have steak, never mind *how* it was cooked!" Zach said.

"Well, that wasn't the greatest challenge of the evening."

"What was?" Zack asked.

"It was the French couple at Table 8."

"Did they speak English?"

"A bit. A tiny bit."

"Do you know French?"

"Sure, I study it at school, but that's more like *La plume de ma tante est sur le bureau de mon oncle*. It's not the same thing as *Comment est-ce qu'on dit 'medium-rare' en français?*"

"So, how *do* you say it?" he asked.

"I don't know. The only thing I could say was *bien cuit*," Jane said.

"What's that?"

"Well-done."

"How'd they like their steaks?" Zach asked.

"They ate every bit."

"Must have liked them."

"I don't think so," Jane said.

"Why?"

"They didn't leave any tip."

"Uh oh. I think you'd better get a French-English dictionary before they come again."

"*If* they come again. Besides that, tomorrow, we'll probably have someone who only speaks Serbo-Croatian." Jane laughed.

"Can't help you there. How about Pig Latin?"

"I never did learn that," Jane admitted.

"How could you *not*?" Zach laughed at her.

"Well, see, I have an older sister who made it her mission in life to be able to say things to her friends that I couldn't understand. So, she never told me how to speak Pig Latin and it was only when I was with her that I needed to know it, so I never asked anybody else."

"Until now."

"I think I'm too old to learn a new language," Jane said.

"Never too old to learn Pig Latin," Zach assured her. "Now here's what you do. You remove the first letter, put it at the end, and add 'ay,' so Zach becomes Ach-Zay. And Jane is Ane-Jay, and so on."

"Swell, I'm sure it'll come in very handy at the restaurant."

"More universal than Serbo-Croatian!"

"Yeah, and wait until I tell Charlotte I know her secret."

"Charlotte?" he echoed.

"Yes, that's my sister.

"Charlotte and Jane. Sounds like Bronte and Austen — very literary."

"Daddy denies it, but I've always suspected Mother chose those names from her favorite authors. Right now, it seems to me that carrying Jane Austen's name is a real challenge."

"You want to be a writer?" Zach asked.

"Oh, yes. I've been taking a creative writing course at school this semester. I've always liked to read and write, but suddenly, it seems like it's all coming together, and it's me."

"I bet you're a wonderful writer," Zach said.

"I've written some things I'm proud of, but I've written some really awful stories, too."

"But you have such a good sense of people," Zach told her.

"What makes you say that?"

"Well, the way you described the mother at the table of fussy eaters."

"But I forgot to tell you the funniest part of the whole story," Jane said.

"Which was . . . ?"

"When the food came."

"Yes?" Zach said, waiting.

"Well, the four kids and the father dug in and ate very contentedly. It was the *mother* who started issuing complaints."

"About her dinner?"

"No, about everybody else's. It was 'My son's steak is too well-done.' 'Ma, it's okay.' 'And can you get more chives for my daughter?' 'I've got enough chives, Mom.' And 'My husband's steak is so small. It looks much smaller than this one.' 'It's big enough for me, Evangeline.' They were *some* group."

Jane and Zach giggled together as they finished their cocoa. Jane was very relaxed and happy. Zach was fun and funny. She could really enjoy herself with him. While they chatted, she thought about the things they had in common: They both loved art, they both enjoyed talking, and laughing, and they laughed at the same things. Being with Zach was easy. Most of the time.

"Come on, Jane. It's late. I've got to get you back home or the Cords will lock me out of lunch tomorrow."

"No way would they do that, but you're right. It is time for me to go. You're so sensible, Zach. I admire that," she said slipping back into her warm coat, hat, and mittens.

"And you're so determined, Jane. I admire that. Waitressing is a tough way to make money, but you're not afraid of that. You know what you have to do and you do it."

Briefly, Jane wondered just how good that was. But then Zach took her hand and led her back out into the night. His presence in the fierce cold was so reassuring that her doubts quickly fled.

CHAPTER TEN

"Pass the ketchup, please!" Ted Cord called down the table. Then, without waiting, he stood up and reached past four people to grab it for himself.

"Speaking of boardinghouse reach!" Mrs. Cord chided good-naturedly. "Pardon my son," she said to Zach, who sat near her.

"It's nothing," he assured her. "My brothers and I will karate chop each other for the last biscuit."

"Well, then it's a good thing I already took it," Charlie teased.

"I'll get some more," Toby offered.

"No, I can get them," Ina Cord said.

"Sit down, Mrs. Cord," Toby said firmly. "I'm closest to the kitchen."

"Thanks, Toby."

"No problem," Toby said, standing up. "Besides, I'm glad for a chance to get out of the melee for just a minute."

The Cords laughed, but Toby was only half-joking. When the kitchen door swung closed behind her, she paused for a moment in contented silence. The din at the Family Lunch was almost too much for her. She could take the whine of winds across the Texas desert. She was comforted by the noises of her father's cattle. But family? She didn't have much and it took some getting used to. Pacing herself, she walked over to the warming oven and loaded the basket with hot biscuits. When she was sure she'd taken as long as she could before they sent out a search party, she went back into the dining room.

The Cords, their cousins, Steve Palmer, Jane, and Zach all burst into applause.

"We're welcoming you back — " Mike Cord explained. "We're glad to have you."

"Not *her* Dad," Charlie interrupted. "It's the *biscuits* we want back."

Toby couldn't help but laugh at this boisterous group as she placed the bread basket on the table in front of Charlie. She shook her head in wonder and asked herself how on earth she could be homesick in the middle of a home like this one? Still, she was.

She picked up her fork and began eating again, watching the family lunch. Zach was sitting next to Jane, but was deep in conversation with Charlie Cord, who sat on his other side, and Ted, who was across the table from him. Mrs. Cord was chatting with her sister, apparently discussing just how much vanilla their mother had put into cakes when they

were little girls. Steve Palmer was seated next
to Andy, but wasn't talking with her at all.
He was talking to Andy's cousins about
whether the White Sox had a chance at the
pennant this year. Andy, in turn was having
an animated conversation with a friend of
Ted's about whether ballet or opera was better value as entertainment. Jane was talking
with Mr. Cord and his brother-in-law about
Chicago restaurants versus Boston restaurants.

Toby could hardly believe all the noise.
She didn't feel left out because she really
didn't want to be a part of the din. She just
felt as if she were watching someone else's
party. Next to her, Andy's two-year-old sister
Nancy sat in her high chair, picking contentedly at a bowl of food. Nancy had aban-
doned her spoon and was selecting strands of
spaghetti. She'd put one end in her mouth
and then, slowly, she'd suck the whole thing
in.

When Nancy's bowl was finally empty,
Toby put a biscuit in front of her. She began
eating that methodically as well. Toby really
admired Nancy's ability to focus only on what
was important to *her*.

"How do you like the thaw we got today?"
Mike Cord asked her.

"Sorry?" Toby said. She hadn't heard him.

"The weather, Toby. Did you notice how
much warmer it got?"

"It seemed pretty cold to me," she said,
dubious.

"Sure it's cold, but it warmed up by thirty degrees. Today it's a relatively mild 23°."

"Sounds like spring!" Charlie joked.

"Not exactly, but we ought to take advantage of it this afternoon," Mr. Cord recommended.

"I know how I'm going to take advantage of this afternoon," Ted said. "I'm going to watch the Bulls' game."

"No, you're not," his mother told him. "It's your turn to look after Nancy while I do the week's menus."

"Aw, Mom," Ted complained.

"Say, I can look after Nancy," Toby offered.

"You don't have to," Ted told her.

"It isn't have to. I'd like to. Since it's so warm out, could I take her for a walk?"

"Well, sure, if we bundle you both up, I don't know why not. Nancy really loves the cold weather," Mrs. Cord said.

"I'd like that, too," Toby said. "I mean I know it's not warm out, but it is sunny, and that would be nice. I kind of like the outdoors, you know — even when you've got it all covered by concrete."

"Nancy likes it, too," Andy told her. "I'll help you both get dressed."

By then, everybody was done with lunch. In a few minutes, the table was cleared and the men, by Family Lunch tradition, were doing the dishes. Within a very few minutes, Nancy and Toby had on enough clothes to get them to the North Pole. Toby put Nancy in her stroller, grabbed her wallet and they went out in search of the park "just three blocks to the left, then take a right, up hill, and you can't miss it."

She could miss it. She did miss it.

"This can't be right, Nancy," Toby told her little charge. "Do *you* know where the park is?"

"Park," was Nancy's answer. "Park there!"

Well, not exactly. Nancy was pointing to a scraggly little tree growing next to a fire hydrant. It didn't really matter to Toby. She was happy walking and Nancy was happy being outside, so they kept walking and being outside.

"See, Nancy," Toby explained. "As long as we keep walking in one direction, then we only have to go in one direction to get back, so we can't get lost, right?"

"Park!" Nancy said, pointing to another tree.

"Right you are, girl!" Toby laughed. "You know, Nancy, it's refreshing to talk to you. You seem to know your own mind and you seem to know what's good for you. You know what you want and you know how to get it. That's more than I can say for my roommates these days!"

Nancy didn't answer.

"I mean, here we have one girl — Jane by name — who is falling all over herself over a guy who is one-hundred percent wrong for her. That guy may be falling in love all right, but he's not falling in love with Jane, because he doesn't know Jane, because she didn't introduce herself yet. Just wait until he finds out who she is. That'll be fireworks."

"Doggie!" Nancy said in response. "See doggie." She was reaching for a Doberman who was sniffing at a nearby tree. The Doberman was three times Nancy's size. It seemed funny that Nancy would still call him "doggie." That sounded like a puppy. This was no puppy. "Doggie!" she insisted. The dog eyed her, hungrily.

The dog's owner tugged at the leash and they moved on. Nancy turned around in her stroller and started barking to call after the dog, but he was gone. "Bowwow! Doggie!"

"Come on, Nancy, you're acting just like Jane. There's no future between you and Fang, there. Forget him."

Toby laughed at the parallel. She continued pushing the stroller, taking the right hand branch when the street divided. At the next fork, she went left.

"And your sister, Nancy. Well, I'm telling you, Andy's no better off than Jane."

"See car! Pretty car."

"Sure, pretty car. There's that Steve Palmer — a perfect match for Andy if I ever saw one — and each is pretending that the other one doesn't exist. Can you believe that?"

"Park!" Nancy pointed to the left. It really was a park.

"I don't know how we got here, but you're right, Nancy. It *is* a park. Let's go."

She turned the stroller into the park and continued walking, this time along the tree-lined paths. The bare black branches reached across the blue sky above. Toby rather liked the bleakness of it. At least the trees weren't concrete.

"You know, Nancy. You're so easy to talk to — almost as easy as talking to Max. I'm sure you understand me as well as he does. Max is my horse, you see. He's my best friend. He and I talk some. I don't usually spend a lot of time talking to people. I think people often spend too much time talking and not enough time at other stuff, but you know what?"

She paused for a response, but Nancy had drifted off to sleep in the stroller.

Toby continued. "In the case of my two friends, I think there's too much other stuff going on and not *enough* talking. I think if they each spent a few minutes talking and not pretending, they'd both be better off. That's what I think. Don't you?"

Nancy didn't answer. Toby was pretty sure Nancy would agree with her.

Suddenly a cold wind whipped at Toby's face. It seemed colder than it had been. Toby glanced at her watch. It was 3:45. She'd left the restaurant at 2:30. That meant she'd been walking — and talking — for over an hour. It also meant she didn't have the slightest idea where she was, where the restaurant was, or where the Cords' apartment was. She stood still and looked around her.

She was in a park. There was a street nearby, but she didn't know what street it was, and even if she did, it wouldn't help because she didn't know where it led to.

She was lost.

In panic, Toby began walking, nearly running. She needed to get some help, but she didn't know where it would be or what she wanted. The park, which had had other people in it, now seemed completely empty. The short winter afternoon was coming to a close and the sky was darkening. She could hear the cars on the street, but they couldn't help her. Nancy was asleep, but even if she understood the problem, she'd be no help getting home.

Toby ran faster.

How could she have let this happen? She was angry with herself. She'd gotten so involved in criticizing her friends' failures with boys that she'd forgotten her own safety, and, worse, the safety of little Nancy.

There had to be a way. Somehow, she'd get help.

Then she saw it. It was a horse, just a bit ahead of her in the park. When Toby reached the horse, she realized that its rider was a policeman. She'd never seen a mounted policeman before, at least not in a city, but she was awfully glad to see him now.

"Oh, officer, I need your help."

"What is it, miss?" he asked politely.

"I've done the dumbest thing. I've gotten myself so lost. I'm here visiting friends and I took their baby out for a walk and I wasn't paying any attention and now I don't know where I am — "

All her misery came flooding out at once. Her eyes brimmed with tears.

"Hold on a second there, miss. Do you know the address of your friends?"

"Well, of course, but I don't know where it is." A tear rolled down her cheek.

The policeman climbed down from his horse and handed her a handkerchief. "I think you'll find that one of the cab drivers at that taxi stand will be able to help you. Do you need some money?" he asked.

Toby was so embarrassed, she could hardly speak. Of course she had money. She was carrying her wallet in her jacket the way she always did.

"No, thank you, officer," she stuttered, returning the handkerchief. "I've got money and I'll take a cab." She told him the Cords' address. "Is that far from here? Will it cost much?"

"No, miss, it is only about ten blocks from here, but you seem cold and if you can take a taxi, I think you should."

"Thank you very much."

"You're welcome. Enjoy the rest of your stay, miss," he said. Toby waved to him and she pushed the stroller out of the park and up to the first cab in line at the taxi stand. How could she have forgotten about taxi stands? Andy had told her that she'd find them every few blocks in the city.

Holding Nancy, Toby folded the stroller and climbed in the taxi, giving the driver the Cord's address.

She relaxed in the back of the cab and thought about what she'd just done. It was actually pretty ironic that she'd panicked until she'd seen a policeman on a horse. It took a horse to give her comfort while all the time the answer to her problem was outside the park on the street. It hadn't even occurred to her to get a taxi, though the answer was obvious to the man on the horse.

"Habits," she told the still-sleeping Nancy. "We develop habits and they get very hard to break. Like I'm in the habit of trusting people on horses, even when that's a silly thing to do. Some habits are good, but some are bad and you can't break bad habits until you know they're bad. Got that, Nancy?"

Nancy stirred on her lap.

"Park! I want to go to the park," she said, pointing to a playground — the playground they'd started out looking for.

"Tomorrow, Nancy. I'll take you to the park tomorrow. That's a promise. Now let's get warm.

"Here you are, Miss," the cab driver said. Toby paid him the money and gave him a big tip. He'd really helped her a lot — even though *he* didn't ride a horse.

CHAPTER
ELEVEN

Y ou were what?" Andy and Jane looked at Toby in total astonishment.

"Like I said, I was saved by a knight in shining armor, riding a white horse. Actually, the horse wasn't white, it was a chestnut and the only thing shining on the knight was his badge, but when you're in a big city, it's hard to come by real knights."

"Boy, trust Toby to find the only horse in Chicago."

"I was sort of thinking the same thing myself," Toby told her friends.

"Luck?" Jane asked her.

"Not really, that's not what I mean. I mean, in my own mind, what I needed to find was something familiar, so when I saw a horse, it was familiar, and that's what helped me. But I'll admit to you, which I wouldn't to that nice policeman, it was really dumb of me not to think of getting a taxi. You see, though, I'm not *used* to getting into taxis. We don't have them in my part of Texas."

"Come on," Jane said. She couldn't imagine life without taxis.

"Well, there's old Ben Juaro, but he's not really a taxi driver. He just hangs around the barber shop and if somebody looks tired, he gives them a lift and if they give him money, it's fine with him. If that's a taxi, then I lied. Anyway, that's not my point. What I mean is that we get used to things. We fall into habits — behavior patterns."

"Wait a minute," Andy interrupted. "You're doing a lot of talking, Toby. That's not like you. You plannng to break your behavior patterns?"

"If you'll give me a chance," Toby snapped.

"Hey, I'm sorry. Really, though, Toby, we're just glad to see you back. We actually were worried."

"I know you were. But I don't think it was me. It was Nancy you were worried about."

"Both of you," Andy assured her. "Now tell us about behavior patterns."

As carefully as she could, Toby outlined her thoughts about the patterns her friends had developed in their relationships with Zach and Steve respectively. She explained how she thought they'd gotten into those grooves and how she thought they ought to get out of them. She explained how much better off each of them would be if they followed her advice.

Andy understood exactly what Toby meant about Jane and Zach. Jane understood perfectly what Toby meant about Andy and Steve. Neither understood what she'd said about themselves.

The big message that got through to Toby, though, was that she should mind her own business. So much for that bright idea, Toby told herself.

"Come on, girls. Time to put on our glamorous uniforms, for even as we speak, tonight's customers are beginning to think about mother's wonderful country-style chicken — tonight's special," Andy said.

"Jane, your order for Table 6 is up," Toby told her.

"And has been for a while," Andy added, a little edgy.

Jane gave her a sharp look and, grabbing a tray, went to the set-up area. Unenthusiastically, she piled the plates on the tray and took them over to Table 6.

"Who's got the medium sirloin?"

"Me," the man with the red shirt told her.

"No, yours was medium-well. Mine's the medium," his wife corrected him.

"No, yours was medium, but it was the porterhouse."

Jane sighed. She knew that if she could reach for her order pad she could tell them who ordered which, but she'd been too lazy to do that when she loaded the tray and she didn't feel like doing it now. She let them bicker. Eventually, they sorted it out.

"Dessert?" she said brightly to Table 5.

"No, we already told you, we want coffee. Do you have any?"

She'd forgotten. Easiest thing in the restaurant to handle and she'd forgotten.

"Coming up," she told them and turned around. "Toby, can you do coffee for Table 5? I'm going to take a break."

"Sure, Jane."

Exhausted, Jane walked to the break table in the kitchen. She poured herself a soda and stared blankly at nothing. Things seemed very confusing to her. She'd been out late with Zach the night before and she'd spent the afternoon with him. He was so interesting. He was so handsome. He liked her so much. Jane was seeing him later that night, too. That was good.

Then there was work. Somehow, it seemed to be going from bad to worse. Back at Canby Hall, this had seemed like a great idea. Andy needed her help. She was going to give it. Now it seemed like trying to help Andy was more work than she had counted on and, in any case, she wasn't being much help. Everytime she turned around, someone else was ready to tell her something else she hadn't done, or that she needed to do immediately, and should have done before, or they wanted to tell her something she ought to have done that they'd done for her. This was no fun at all.

The part Jane couldn't understand was how well Andy could do the job. Then there was

Toby. Toby was just as new at this as she was, but she could do it, too.

What is wrong with me? Jane wondered.

Jane rested her chin in her hands to think. Her eyes closed.

"Hey Jane!" It was a whisper, but it was nearby. Jane was startled. "Jane! Don't let Mrs. Cord see you sleeping," Toby said gently.

"Sleeping?"

"Yeah, for about a half hour, but I covered. It's okay. Come on, pardner. Let's finish up."

It took all of Jane's strength to stand up and walk back into the dining room.

"Why don't you skip the date tonight with Zach tonight?" Toby suggested.

"Give me a break, Toby. Looking forward to that is the only thing that's going to keep me awake the rest of the evening."

"Hmph," Toby said, hoping it sounded neutral, and changed the subject. "Uh, Table 8 needs to be cleared."

"Oh, Zach, this is really something."

"Having trouble, Janie?" He reached out and held her hand comfortingly.

"I don't know, sometimes it seems like it's just too much for me."

They were sitting across from each other in the booth at the all-night diner. The thick white cups with cocoa cooled in front of them.

"Well, Jane, I know you and I know you're giving it absolutely everything you've got."

"I don't know that, Zach," Jane said, truthfully. "I mean, if I were, I'd be able to *do* the job, wouldn't I? I know I'm able to do all kinds of work, but this — this is really wearing me down."

"Jane," Zach said. "Let's be sensible. This is a mistake."

Jane got a queasy feeling. "Mistake?"

"Yeah, we have no business having late dates when you've got a taxing job to do. I'm taking you home now. You get a good night's sleep and everything will look better in the morning — or whenever you wake up. I'm going to be busy all day tomorrow anyway so I can't see you then. You just have a restful day and by tomorrow night, this job will be a breeze, right?"

"Maybe," Jane told him. Still, she wasn't sorry to be returning to the Cords'. She was ready to collapse.

It didn't make sense to her, though. She was getting ten hours of sleep a night. That ought to be enough. Why was she so tired?

Within a very few minutes, Jane was back at the Cords' apartment. Toby and Andy were sleeping. Silently, Jane slipped into her pajamas and climbed into her bed. For a long time, she stared at the light patterns on the ceiling, reflections off the blinds from the street below. Knowing something was wrong and knowing how to right it were definitely two different things.

Finally, she slept.

CHAPTER TWELVE

"Here, Toby, have another cup of tea and tell me again about this recipe."

Ina Cord spoke earnestly, eagerly. She poured the tea for Toby and Andy, who sat at the kitchen table in the Cord apartment. It was eleven o'clock in the morning. Jane was still sleeping soundly—apparently needing the rest.

"Well, it's just chili," Toby said.

"Nothing is 'just chili' where my mother is concerned," Andy explained. "Chili is just about the most argued-about food in the cooking business."

"But chili's chili," Toby said.

"Ah, but *what's* chili?" Mrs. Cord asked, somewhat illogically.

"Chili's what we have for mess every Friday night on the ranch."

"Beans in it?"

"Of course."

"Ground meat or chunks?" Ina quizzed.

"Chunks, of course."

"Could you make a batch for us so I could taste it?"

"I suppose," Toby said. "Problem is, we only make it when there are going to be forty or fifty people around. I'm not sure I could make it for just a few."

A great big smile came to Mrs. Cord's face.

"What makes you so happy about that?" Toby asked.

"Toby, child," Ina began. "On New Year's Eve — that's tomorrow night — we've got about two hundred and fifty people coming for a party. It's one of the biggest parties we've had at the restaurant. Usually when we have a banquet, they want chicken or steak. What I want to serve for dinner is chili. Chili is, actually, a near-perfect meal for a big group of people — forty or fifty, as you say — or two hundred and forty or fifty. So this is a real opportunity to show off. Now I make chili. And I make it good. But I've always wondered if there weren't something I could do to it to make it *great*."

"Oh, that's easy," Toby assured her. Mrs. Cord reached for paper and pencil and, as Toby explained what she remembered of the process the ranch cook used, Ina Cord made notes.

Andy got up from the kitchen table and put her breakfast dishes in the sink. She knew from experience that when her mother was working on a cooking project, she'd be busy for hours. Therefore, so would Toby. Andy returned to her room to wake Jane up and to get dressed for the day. It was going to be a good day for Andy, a special day.

"Good morning, Jane," Andy said cheerfully.

Jane opened one eye. She closed it.

"I know you're in there," Andy told her.

"Hmmph." At least it was a response.

"I've got a plan, Jane."

Both eyes opened. Andy handed her an extra pillow. Jane propped herself up and looked attentive. "Yeah?"

"There's a matinée performance of the ballet this afternoon. Students' half-price tickets are available. They go on sale in an hour. The performance is at two. It'll be over in time to get to the restaurant for dinner. You and I could have lunch downtown before the performance, after we get our tickets."

It sounded pretty good to Jane. "What about Toby?" she asked. "She coming, too?"

"Mom and Toby are going to have a chili cook-off. They'll be doing that all afternoon. Ballet?"

"You bet," Jane said, stumbling out of bed. "I'll be ready in a minute."

"Relax. No need to rush," Andy said. "Three minutes will do."

Jane smiled. "Thanks, Andy. You're a pal." Jane headed for the kitchen for some breakfast while Andy showered.

The afternoon at the ballet gave both Andy and Jane an opportunity to do something they hadn't done together since Jane had arrived. They had fun. Andy was near euphoric about the ballet and Jane simply enjoyed it. For four hours, neither one thought about work or boyfriends. They thought about ballet and each other.

After the performance, they took the bus back to the restaurant.

"I really liked that," Jane said.

"Wasn't it wonderful? Didn't you just love the lead ballerina? And, oh, her *jetés*. It seemed like she floated across the stage — like there was no floor there at all. You know how hard that is to do? I've tried it. Boy, have I. When I see a performance like that, you know, it's humbling. I love ballet so and I know that's what I want to do — am doing, really — but when you see someone that good, you just know how much harder and longer you have to work."

Jane listened idly while staring out the dirty window of the el. As they got closer to the restaurant, Jane could feel the tension building up in herself. Andy chattered on.

" — and the *costumes* — didn't you love the sparkling rainbow colors? You know, people used to think dancers *had* to wear tutus, but that's not true at all. Some of the best costumes today are not tutus, but then there are times when you really *need* tutus. Don't you think so? Jane?" Andy looked at her friend and saw that her mind was somewhere else.

"Jane, what's up? Something bothering you?"

"Oh, I don't know."

"Come on, tell," Andy invited her.

"It's just that, well, I was thinking about the night ahead of us."

"It's getting easier for you now, isn't it?" Andy asked.

Suddenly, all the happiness and relaxation of the pleasant afternoon was washed away by a flood of anger. "No," she said to Andy. "It's not getting easier. Every night is harder and less fun than the last. It's supposed to get easier. It's easier for Toby, and for you, but not for me."

"It will, Jane, I promise. It's just a matter of getting used to it." Andy tried to calm her. It didn't work.

"I'm not getting used to it. I keep thinking I will, but I don't."

"Jane, are you sure it's the work at the restaurant that's bothering you? Could it be something else?"

"Like what?" Jane challenged her.

"Oh, like maybe, uh, I don't know." She did know. Andy was pretty sure it was Zach that was Jane's problem, but she also knew that Jane would be deaf to such a suggestion so she didn't suggest it. "Maybe you're worried about the chili?"

Jane stared at her in astonishment and then burst out laughing. "I'm *sure* that's it." She shook her head ruefully. "Now, tell me about this big deal party on New Year's Eve."

"Well, New Year's Eve is always fun. It's like the whole restaurant is one big party. In a way, it's harder than other nights, but it's easier, too, because everybody's so cheerful. Dad's got a country rock band coming and there'll be dancing after dinner. Once we're done serving and cleaning up, we can join the party. It's always a lot of fun."

"If the chili's good?"

"Right." Andy laughed. "Here's our stop."

Together, they left the train and headed for the restaurant.

For Jane, the night was a marked contrast to the wonderful afternoon she'd had with Andy at the ballet. It started out all right. She was teamed with Steve and for a while everything went very smoothly. For the first time, she began to feel she knew what she was doing. She didn't mix up orders, she didn't forget who was in a rush, who wanted their sour cream on the side, who needed their steak salt-free, who ordered the secret surprise birthday cake for which customer. She did it all. It was very satisfying to her, but then it started to sour.

The first sign that the evening was going sour was when she added up a bill wrong.

Jane tried to be super-careful about her math. She always used the calculator but, in this case, she'd pushed the wrong buttons.

"Miss!" the customer snapped at her. She

went to the table. "You've made a mistake here." He pointed to the check.

"I'm sorry, sir, let me have a look."

"You doubt me?" He asked.

"Oh, no, it's not that, I just — "

"You're not going to get away with this, you know?"

"Get away with it?" she asked.

"I know when I'm being cheated."

"Cheated?" she repeated, astonished.

"You're denying it?"

"Oh, no, I mean, I didn't mean — "

He cut her off. "You don't deny you were cheating me?"

Jane could hardly believe the conversation she was having, or really wasn't having with this man. She was so flustered she could hardly speak. He raised his voice until he was nearly yelling. Jane was frantic and didn't know what to do, until Mr. Cord finally appeared at her side.

"What's the problem here?" he asked calmly, politely. As suddenly as the man's fury had erupted, it quieted.

"No problem," he said. "It's just that there's a mathematical error on my bill."

"I'll see to it that it's corrected," Mr. Cord assured him, retrieving the bill from the man and returning, with Jane, to the calculator.

"Mr. Cord, I'm so *sorry*," she began.

Quickly, he corrected the error and returned the check to her to take back to the table. Before she left, though, he spoke. "Jane, anybody can make a mistake on a bill. It happens. What shouldn't happen is letting it get out of hand. At his first harsh word, you should have called me over. Understand?"

"Yes. I'm sorry."

"It's okay." He smiled encouragingly. Jane didn't feel encouraged.

Then Steve asked her to serve Table 14. She picked up a tray of food and took it over to the station nearest 14. She unveiled the plates and picked one up in each hand.

"Who ordered the ribs?" she asked.

They looked at her blankly. She looked at the plate closely. It *was* ribs. Maybe there had been a mix-up in the kitchen.

"Okay, then who ordered chicken in a basket?"

"Nobody," one of the diners said. "We all ordered steak."

"Oops, sorry," she said, embarrassed, putting the plates back on the tray. She realized that she'd picked up the wrong tray of food. That was bad, but what was worse was that one of her friends was across the room, trying to sell steak to the chicken and ribs eaters.

When that was finally sorted out, there was something else. By then, it seemed to Jane that there was always something else. This time, it was two customers, dining together, who got into a big argument. Jane had no idea what they were arguing about, but when she tried to calm them down, they both got angry at *her*. Once again, Mr. Cord came to her rescue. After he had calmed them down by politely asking them to leave, he spoke to Jane again, reminding her that she should have asked for his help.

"I didn't want to bother you," she explained.

"It's no bother," he told her. "It's what I'm here for. This is my place; these are my customers and I want them to come back — except for that pair."

Jane was terribly discouraged. She knew how important the restaurant was to the Cords and she also knew how quickly bad service could empty a place. It seemed to her that she was a good deal more trouble than she was help. When Michael Cord told her to take a break, she was pretty sure he just wanted her out of the way so she wouldn't goof anything else up and ruin his business. Glumly, she headed for the staff table in the kitchen and sat — too upset even to pour herself a soda.

Things didn't get better when Zach called, either. Suddenly, she realized that she couldn't take his sympathy. He was so sure he understood her — much better than she did herself — and she wasn't at all certain he was right.

"Oh, Janie," he said tenderly. "I was so sure you'd be better by now. I just know these people are working you too hard. There's too much pressure on you."

Was there, she asked herself? She really didn't know. She did know that the job she was doing wasn't good enough. She also knew that Barretts don't fall. Those two facts just didn't fit together and it made Jane very uncomfortable.

"I can't talk now, Zach," she told him.

"I know, you're busy, but I just wanted to cheer you on," he told her. She wasn't cheered.

"Good-night," she said, and sat down again at the staff table to think.

By the end of her break, an idea had begun to grow in her mind. Maybe it was a good idea. A little cheered, she returned to work and as she worked, she thought about her idea.

"Can you get coffee for Table 13?" Steve asked her.

"Sure," she agreed. "Table 12 is ready to order."

"I've already got their order," he said.

Wasn't that typical, she thought to herself as she poured coffee for Table 13. She discovered that Table 12 wanted to order and by then, Steve had already taken their order. She thought more about her idea.

Then she was caught in the whirl of her own responsibilities. Relish. Coffee. Check. Serve. Clear. Smile, nod, thank you, goodnight. Come again, now. 'Bye.

Then it was time for desserts at Table 5. They all ordered the house special, Brown Derbies, chewy brownies with a scoop of chocolate ice cream, topped with fudge sauce and whipped cream. She had six of them on her tray. She balanced it very carefully on her hand and her shoulder. She watched the level of the tray carefully — too carefully to notice the glob of butter on the floor. Her foot landed on it and then slid right out from under her.

The tray tipped and while Jane headed for the floor, the tray's contents were delivered, very suddenly, to the table. Some of the six brownies, six scoops of chocolate ice cream, six ladles of fudge sauce, six tops of whipped cream and six plates, landed on the table. The rest got delivered directly — onto six sticky, gooey, unhappy customers.

It was at that point, sitting miserably on the floor, surrounded by the chocolate mess, that Jane made up her mind.

She would go home.

CHAPTER THIRTEEN

Jane, are you sure there isn't something we can do?"

"No, really, I've got everything ready to go."

"That's not what Andy meant, Jane," Toby told her. "We don't want to help you leave. We want to convince you *not* to leave."

"Too late," Jane told her. "And it's not your fault anyway. There's nothing to be said. I made a mistake. I just can't take it and I'm going home."

"You're running away, Jane," Andy said.

"So? The reason I came in the first place was to help. I'm not helping. There's no point in sticking around; I'm just in the way."

"Oh, Jane," Andy said, disappointed. "We all make mistakes. Yours aren't any worse than anyone else's."

"You didn't splatter brown derbies all over absolutely everyone, did you?"

"No, actually, the time I did that, it was with spaghetti. Tomato sauce really stains badly, too," Andy told her.

"And I did it with a variety of main courses," Toby reminded her. "The chocolate sauce everywhere was really much funnier than the main courses." She and Andy giggled in recollection of the gigantic mess Jane had made. Jane didn't laugh.

"Where's my cashmere sweater?" she asked.

"You already stuffed it into the suitcase."

"No, that was the lamb's wool," Jane corrected her.

"Here's the cashmere," Andy found it.

"I'm out of room in my suitcase. I'll have to shove it into my handbag," Jane said.

"Along with this," Andy handed her her Texas cowhide wallet. "And this." She gave Jane her large silk scarf which seemed to be knotted around some other stuff. Jane jammed it into her bag.

"And here is your ticket," Toby said. "See, I knew we'd be able to help you. I just wish you'd stay."

"It's just one more night, Jane, and it's the big New Year's Eve party."

"With *my* chili recipe," Toby said proudly.

"Friends, it's time for me to go home. I'll see you back at school on Monday."

"Nothing we can say or do?" Andy asked.

"Nothing," Jane said with finality. "Goodbye. I'm sorry, I've made such a mess of things."

Just then, the doorbell rang. It was Zach. He had borrowed his mother's car and had volunteered to take Jane out to the airport.

Jane felt a little uneasy about that. She knew that, in leaving Chicago, she was, as a practical matter, saying good-bye to Zach — at least until he came to visit his father in Boston again. Still, she felt her decision was a good one. Some experiments don't work. Her experiment in waitressing was a failure. It was time to walk away from it.

"Zach's here," Ina Cord called into Andy's room.

"I'll be right there," Jane said.

"Jane, you forgot your makeup kit," Toby told her, retrieving it from the bathroom.

"And here's your pajama top," Andy said, pulling it out of the mess of blankets on the bed.

"Back to the upstairs maid?" Toby asked, but Jane still wasn't up to teasing, and Toby wasn't really teasing. Jane took the things her friends handed her and stuffed them into her carry-on, oversized handbag. Quickly, she hugged her friends, sensing the distance between them. Then she left the room.

Zach took her suitcase down to the car while she said good-bye and thank you to the Cords, all of whom were in the kitchen. After the uncomfortable farewells, Jane left. Long after the sound of her footsteps had echoed away, baby Nancy stood by the door, waving and saying " 'Bye 'bye Jane. 'Bye 'bye Jane."

Toby and Andy sat at the kitchen table with the rest of the family.

"Boy, she really is running away, isn't she?" Andy asked.

"Sure is," Mrs. Cord said. "Problem is that she doesn't know what she's running *from*, and believe me if you don't know where you want to go, no airplane's going to get you there."

"I didn't think she was all that bad as a waitress," Ted said.

"Certainly no worse than *you* are," Charlie teased him.

"You know, you're right, Charlie. You too, Ted. Jane is pretty good," Mike Cord said. "I had my doubts about both Jane and Toby, as you know, but I was wrong. Toby's almost as good as Andy, and Jane's nearly that good. She works hard and she cares a lot about what she does. Last night, a really unpleasant man started accusing her of trying to cheat him with the bill. She tried very hard to handle that herself — and, with another customer, she probably would have succeeded."

"Wasn't she also on the table with that awful couple that were fighting so loudly?"

"Yes," Mr. Cord nodded. "Jane tried to make peace with them, too, but there was no way to silence them. She was very ambitious. I admire that."

"Well, she's gone now," Toby said.

"Yes, she is. And we'll miss her tonight," Andy added.

"Oh, yes," Mrs. Cord said. "And speaking of tonight, Toby you've got to come with me to the market now to get supplies for the chili. I hope we can get all the fresh stuff your cook uses."

"Well, if not, we'll just make do with what we have."

"Swell. Experimental chili for dinner," Ted moaned. Charlie laughed.

"Ted," Toby said patiently. "Chili is *always* experimental. That's why it's always good. Count on it."

"I will," he assured her. "We all will."

With that, the Cords and Toby went back to work.

A few miles away, Zach turned onto the Expressway, following signs to O'Hare International Airport.

"Want to tell me about it?" he said to Jane.

"I don't suppose there's much to tell," she evaded.

"They just worked you too hard?"

"I guess so."

"Guess so?" he challenged her.

"Well, sort of. I mean, Zach, it was too much for me. I tried. I really tried. Again and again."

"I know you did, Janie. I know how much of yourself you put into it. I just want to try to understand."

"Me, too."

"I'm disappointed, too, you know."

"I know," she said. But she didn't really. It was funny how Zach made her feel. At first, it had seemed so wonderful — and he was wonderful to her. Always there, always supportive, always caring about her.

"I'll be in Boston again at Easter time. I'll see you then."

"Yeah," Jane agreed. Then she thought about Easter at home. And she thought about her home. It was one thing to go along with Zach's perceptions of her as a hardworking poor girl, when she was staying with friends in Chicago. It was another when she'd be in her own home, a four-story town house in Lowsburg Square. It was very different from the apartment in Chicago where the Cords lived. Maybe she could convince him that her mother was a maid in their house. She thought of how her mother would react to that. She started laughing to herself.

"What's so funny?"

"Oh, nothing. I was just thinking about home."

"It'll be nice to be home, huh? Be it ever so humble?"

"I guess so."

"What time is your flight? This traffic is pretty bad, stop and go. I'd like to be sure we've got enough time, Janie."

She wished he'd stop calling her Janie. It

seemed so undignified, but she didn't say anything. There was no point. "Um, I'll check my ticket."

She leaned forward and started rummaging through her carry-on.

He glanced as the makeup kit came out and went onto the seat between them. Then the sweater. Jane shoved the pajama tops under the sweater.

"Sorry," she said, embarrassed.

"Pack in a hurry?" he asked.

"Sort of."

She pulled out her wallet. It was the Texas cowhide wallet Toby had given her for Christmas. She swallowed hard, remembering the happiness of that party in Room 407. It seemed so long ago now, but it was only two weeks ago. Seventeen days. Jane set those memories aside. The catch to a necklace had gotten caught in the wallet. Jane tugged at that. Out came her comb and some papers in envelopes. The ticket wasn't in any of the envelopes.

She pulled out the silk scarf she'd worn on her way to the airport in Boston. It had wrapped itself around a lot of the junk in her carry-on, including her ticket. Carelessly, she pushed the scarf and its contents onto the seat between herself and Zach, and turned her attention to the wrinkled ticket in her hand. She'd jotted her new flight number onto the back of it when she made the reservation.

"Four-fifteen," she said, triumphantly.

"Okay, we've got plenty of time. At least we have plenty of time to get to the airport." The car was stopped in traffic for a moment. He glanced at the pile of things she'd removed from her bag. "I'm not sure we have enough for you to repack all that junk into your carry-on bag. How can you have such a mess?"

"I'm just that way, Zach. I'm not organized with my personal belongings. Never have been." Jane was matter-of-fact about it. Zach shook his head disapprovingly as she tried to stuff the things back.

"Don't do it that way," he advised her. "Separate the things and put them back in some order. That way, next time you want the ticket, you don't have to pull out your pajama tops."

"Okay," she relented. Then she reached for the scarf and its contents and began shoving it back in.

"Not like that," he said, a little annoyed that she was ignoring him. "Look, get this stuff out of there." The car was stopped again so Zach could help Jane. He took the scarf out of her hands and shook it to let out the things she'd rolled into it. Jane tried to stop him, but it was too late.

What landed on the seat was her own American Express Gold credit card, and her mother's store credit cards for Lord & Taylor, Neiman-Marcus, and Marshall Field's.

"What's this?" Zach asked, surprised.

"Oh, nothing," Jane said, reaching for the cards.

"No, it's not nothing," he corrected her. "These are credit cards. Where did you get them?"

"Uh, Zach, it's a long story. Let me try to explain — "

"I'll bet there's a lot to explain." His voice was full of righteous fury.

"I didn't even use them," she said, and then wondered why she said that.

"Well, that's a good thing, isn't it. But the crime isn't using them. The crime is in taking them in the first place. Is this why you're leaving Chicago? You want to be gone before someone reports the theft?"

"Theft?" Then Jane realized that Zach thought she'd stolen them from one of the customers at the restaurant. How could he possibly think she would do something like that? "I didn't steal those, Zach."

"What'd you do, buy them from someone? That's the same as stealing, Janie."

"No, Zach, I didn't buy them. They're mine. At least one is. The others are my mother's, but we both use the accounts."

"The accounts?" he echoed. Then he picked up the Marshall Field's card and read *Mrs. David Quincy Barrett*. He turned it over and read the signature, *Gloria Barrett*. " 'David Quincy Barrett' as in David Q. Barrett, Investment Bankers? 'Gloria Barrett' as in Curator of the Barrett Collection?''

Jane nodded.

"Jane, you lied to me," he accused her.

"I suppose it seems that way."

"You told me you were working class, just like me."

"No, Zach, I told you I was working. You decided I was okay, so I had to be working *class* just like you."

"So *that's* why you're going home."

"So *what's* why I'm going home?"

"You're a spoiled little rich girl and you can't do an honest day's work." He grasped the steering wheel tightly as he maneuvered through the traffic.

"That's not true at all and that's not fair," Jane said hotly.

"So what *is* true?" he challenged her.

"What's true is that I was trying very hard to do my work and my best wasn't good enough."

"For the Cords? Did they fire you?" Zach asked.

"No, of course not. It wasn't good enough for *me*." Jane clenched her hands in her lap.

"I'm not sure I know *what* your standards are," he taunted.

All of a sudden the reality of Jane's terrible mistake came rushing over her. Her pent up anger and frustration at her misguided relationship with Zach surged out in fury. "Well,

I'll tell you this, Zach. My standards are higher than yours. You've got a chip on your shoulder so big, it can be seen from a mile away. You've got some things to learn."

"Such as?"

"Just because a person's rich doesn't mean they're no good. There are a lot of rich people who have worked very hard for what they have."

"Easy enough for you to say. All your family's money is inherited."

"I didn't ask for it."

"But you got it, didn't you?"

"What's it to you?"

"Nothing. And you're nothing to me. You're not at all what I thought you were." He drove into the entrance to the airport.

"I know that, Zach." It was her turn for righteous indignation. "And it has nothing to do with money. At first I thought you were the greatest thing I ever saw, but now I know that you couldn't possibly like me for what I am. If what I am isn't good enough for you, then that's your problem. Not mine."

At that moment, Zach pulled up to the curb at the departure area. Quickly, Jane stuffed the rest of her belongings into her carry-on bag and stepped out of the car. Without Zach's help, she pulled her suitcase from the backseat and slammed the doors. He drove off without saying good-bye.

And that was okay, too.

CHAPTER FOURTEEN

Jane tugged her suitcase into the bustling warmth of O'Hare Airport. Once inside, she stood and looked around to orient herself. She saw dozens of signs; none of them made much sense to her at that moment. She had never been more confused in her life and signs directing her to the "A Concourse" or "Pre-Flight Lounges," seemed fairly meaningless.

Still stuffing her things back into her carry-on, she spotted an empty bench that looked pretty inviting. She hauled her luggage over to it and sat down.

Jane had always thought that airports had an electrifying excitement to them. People going places. Different places. New experiences. Old friends. Holidays, vacations. Fun.

If that was going on at O'Hare at that moment, Jane certainly didn't know about it. She sat, motionless, on the bench and stared blankly into space — something she realized she'd been doing a lot recently. She sat up with a start.

"Hey, girl," she told herself in her most common-sense-Ina-Cord voice. "It's time to get down to cases and figure out what's *really* going on in your head." She decided not to stare into space, but to stare into facts.

In her mind, she went over everything that happened since she'd arrived in Chicago — since she'd left Boston, really, because, after all, it was on the plane that she'd met Zach. She'd never known anyone who so completely misjudged her as Zach had. It was as if he wanted her to be something and, regardless of what the facts were, he'd decided that was what she was. And the worst part, Jane realized, was that she'd gone along with him.

Zach absolutely couldn't see below the surface of anyone to see the person who was inside. It wouldn't have mattered to Zach if she'd been the most wonderful girl in the world or second rate; as long as he thought she wasn't rich, she was wonderful to him.

"That's crazy," she said.

" 'Scuse me?"

Jane realized she'd spoken aloud.

"Sorry," she apologized to the woman sitting next to her. "I guess I'm just talking to myself."

"Are you listening, too?" the woman asked, smiling.

"I hope so," Jane answered and then went back to her own thoughts.

So much for Zach, she told herself. Boy, was I ever a fool. And my friends tried to tell me. They did. But I wasn't listening. I was just thinking about that good-looking boy. And she thought about him again. She could see his serious eyes and the curly brown hair and the straight nose and the beautiful mouth, with the smile. Oh, that smile. But that's all there was. The rest of him was all wrong for me and I didn't see it.

And then she realized that that was crazy, too. What she had done to Zach was no better and no worse than what he had done to her.

But what had she done to her friends? she asked herself. She thought about Ina and Mike Cord, Charlie, Ted, and baby Nancy. She thought about how hard they had worked to make her feel at home, to teach her something about their business, to welcome her friend at their table. She thought about Toby and Andy. It was Andy she had come to help in the first place. Some help she'd been and now she'd left them — all of them — in the lurch, the night before they'd need her the most, New Year's Eve. How could she do that to friends?

I've got two of the best friends in the world. They weren't even angry with me when I was making a complete nerd of myself over Zach. How could I do this to them? How can

I face them at school on Monday? she thought.

Jane stood up. She needed to walk to get her thinking straightened out. She held her coat over one arm, along with her overstuffed carry-on. With the other, she pulled her suitcase.

It was frightening to her to think what she would say when they returned to school. Maybe she could move into another room. Maybe she ought to drop out of school.

And run away again? she asked herself. Again? For that, she realized, was what she was doing now. She was running away.

Barretts don't quit. We don't run away from our problems. We face them.

Then Jane knew what the answer was. Hard as it would be for her, she had to go back. In the long run, it would be a lot easier than running away. She had two good friends in Toby and Andy. She wanted to keep it that way. Because Jane plus Andy plus Toby equaled friends times three.

She turned to look for the door. The place was full of doors, but she needed one that would get her to a taxi. She had to hurry, too. It was almost four o'clock and by the time she got back to the restaurant, the early customers would be arriving for the New Year's Eve party.

Then she spotted the exit to the taxi stand. She probably would have made it to the door in time to get the lone taxi there if only her suitcase hadn't suddenly popped open. Within seconds, every piece of clothing in it was strewn across twenty yards of O'Hare.

Busy, rushing travelers began retrieving her things for her.

"Here's a sweater — "

"This your skirt, miss?"

"Here's your lipstick. Nice shade."

Jane wished, more than anything, that the floor could open up and swallow her. Her cheeks flushed a bright red of embarrassment as she accepted the kindness of strangers.

"I got a left shoe!" came a triumphant cry.

"Here's the right one!"

Then two very tall young men delivered them. Jane, near tears, thanked them.

"Don't cry, miss," one of the boys told her. "It's not so bad, and it's nearly cleaned up. Look, here's some more stuff," he said, accepting some more clothes for Jane. "If we can't help you get that thing closed, but good, nobody can."

"Huh?" was all Jane could manage.

"Here's the last of it," another boy said. By then, six of them were gathered around her suitcase.

"Okay, miss, say what's your name?"

"Jane."

"Okay, Jane, now you're packed, and we'll close it."

The boys finished stuffing all her belongings

into the suitcase and then three of them together put enough weight on it to close it,
very tightly.

"You just packed it the same way I did," she
told them, laughing for the first time in sev-
eral days, and feeling much better for it.

"We're good at that," the first one said.

"Well, thanks. But since you know me, I
think I ought to know who you are so I can
thank you properly."

"Well, I'm Dan, he's Bob, but we call him
Lobber because of the way he lobs the shots
into the baskets from across the court. That
one's Sid, but he's called Everest." A quick
look at the extremely tall boy explained the
reason for his nickname. "This guy's Rebound Pete. He's Buck — as in Buckingham
Palace because he's a guard. And, finally, this
one's PeeWee, because he's so short." Jane
glanced at PeeWee. He was well over six feet,
but compared to the rest of the crew, he *was*
short.

"A basketball team?" Jane asked.

"At your service," Dan said, and they all
bowed.

"Well, thanks for your help, guys, but you
all have too many names for me to remember
them."

"Well, we all answer to 'Tex' if that's easier," Bob suggested.

"You're from Texas?" Jane asked.

"Yes, indeed, and that's where we're headed,

but for now we're stranded in Chicago. Our charter plane has a damaged engine and we're stuck here. Say, maybe you could help us. The company's putting us up in a hotel, but we'd like to have something to do tonight. You know where we could have a nice time in Chicago? Maybe a New Year's Eve party?"

"I think I might be able to help you," Jane told them, nodding. "You guys like chili? Real *Texas* chili?"

"You bet we do!"

"Then let's get us a couple of taxis, Tex." She looked up at them. "Make that a *fleet* of taxis. I know just the place for you guys!"

CHAPTER FIFTEEN

"Mom, we've just gotten sixteen more reservations," Andy called to her mother and Toby in the kitchen. "Got enough food for them all?"

"Relax, Andy," Toby said calmly. "We've got enough chili bubbling here to feed half of Texas."

"Make that *all* of Texas, Toby, because I think they're here!" She stared out the window at the taxis which just pulled up at the curb. Out stepped six of the tallest young men she'd ever seen off a basketball court. They were attired in cowboy boots, ten gallon hats and, accompanied by —

"Jane!" Andy yelled. "Toby, it's Jane, she's back!"

Toby came running out of the kitchen, garbed in an oversized apron, which was smeared with chili ingredients.

"It *is* Jane!"

Both girls ran out of the restaurant into the

cold evening to greet Jane with welcoming hugs.

Jane was flooded with relief to see them and to know that they were glad to see her.

"Oh, Jane, we're so glad to see you. We're glad you're back. To stay, right?"

"Right!" Jane assured them.

Toby turned her gaze upward and noticed Jane's escorts. "Who are *they?*" she asked.

"Let's get inside and I'll introduce everyone. It's a long story — "

"But a good one?" Andy asked.

"A very good one," Jane assured her.

Within a few minutes, all the suitcases had been extracted from the taxis. The drivers were paid, and the whole group was gathered around a large table in the restaurant.

"Everybody, I'd like you to meet Tex," Jane said.

"Which one is Tex?" Toby asked suspiciously.

"They *all* are," Jane said. "I mean, they've all got other names, lots of 'em, but I've been told that they all answer to Tex and, so far, it's true. Right, Tex?"

"Right," they answered in chorus.

"Now, where's this chili you were talking about?" Tex asked.

"It's right in here," Toby said. "Can't you smell it?"

"Well, sure, but it doesn't smell right. You put the cumin in yet?"

"Cumin! Of course," Toby said. *"That's*

what I forgot. You got any other ideas?"

It turned out that each of the boys had a favorite ingredient in "real Texas chili," and each wanted to tell Ina Cord just how to make it. They all trooped into the kitchen to help.

"Don't worry, girls," Toby told her friends. "Chili is the one food in the world that too many cooks can't spoil." Toby followed the Texans into the kitchen.

Andy turned to her friend, Jane. "Come on, let's put your stuff away and get ready for the party." She picked up Jane's bag and started to walk into the dressing room. But then she stopped and spoke again. "Oh, Jane, I'm so glad you're back."

"I'm so glad to *be* back, Andy. I made such an idiot of myself over Zach, but I know better now. I've learned something, a lot in fact. I'm just awfully sorry about the nuisance I've been."

"Don't spend any time worrying about *that*. It's over and you're back and that's what's important. Later on, you can tell us what happened."

"Actually, it was pretty funny," Jane told her. "And it's all because I'm such a slob." While Jane dressed, she told Andy about her suitcase bursting open and her clothes being scattered all over the airport. By the time she had her uniform on, they were both laughing helplessly at Jane's description of the scene. "What really frosted it was when that lady ad-

mired the color of my lipstick. Oh, Andy, it
was *something*. I wish you'd been there."

"I'm glad I wasn't."

"Yeah, but look what I got out of it."

"Six giant Texas sidekicks. Toby must be
in seventh heaven in the kitchen."

"Let's go see."

"Right on, pardner!" Andy agreed.

New Year's Eve was different from any other
night at Steak 'n Ribs. Instead of the usual
restaurant set-up, it was like one big party.
There was no menu. Everybody had the same
thing to eat: chili with all the fixings, salad,
corn bread, and plenty of butter. There was a
band coming to play country rock music when
dinner was over. They'd push the tables back
against the wall, leaving a large dance floor
in the center of the room. Dinner would be
served at eight o'clock, the dancing would
start at ten and go on until nobody could
stand up anymore. After dinner, the staff
could join the dancers, so by midnight everyone would be in on the party.

Jane, Andy, and Toby had to work quickly
to set up the restaurant for the crowd that
would start arriving by seven. Between eight
and ten, everybody would eat, so everything
had to be ready.

Fortunately, because of Jane, they had six
able-bodied assistants who were only too glad
to be able to help shift the tables around.

"I never saw a better crew," Mike Cord said.

"That's how we got here in the first place, helping Jane with her luggage," one of them said.

"Got any other suitcases for us to close?"

"Not tonight. Just relax and enjoy yourselves, boys," Mr. Cord told them. "And, when the dancing starts, we expect you Texans to show the Northerners just how to kick up our heels to Country-Western music."

"Glad to help out, sir," Buck said.

Then the guests arrived. As before, they worked in teams. This time, Toby and Jane were one team, Andy and Steve were another. And, as never before, they *were* teams. Jane could hardly believe how smoothly things could go when her mind wasn't completely occupied with making a fool of herself and lying to Zach.

"More water for the big group in the corner," she told Toby.

"Right on. Oh, and the pair at Table 12 just asked for seconds on chili."

"Better tell one of the Texans about that. They think they made the whole batch," Jane said.

"They did. The batch Mrs. Cord and I made was sold out already."

"Good thing I dumped my suitcase in the airport, huh?"

"Good thing you came back," Toby corrected her.

"Actually, the good thing was getting myself squared away about Zach. Now, if only we could do something about Andy and Steve."

"Tell me about it," Toby said. Together, the girls watched the other team work the other half of the dining room. "Look at them, working side by side and still acting like each doesn't know the other exists."

"It's all an act on Steve's part, you know," Jane said.

"Yeah, I know. How do we get them off the stage and into each other's arms?"

"We keep our mouths shut," Jane said.

"I know you're right," Toby agreed, reluctantly. "Oops, Table 6 is ready for dessert."

"You do that; I'll clear Table 8."

" 'Bye."

"Steve, how do you manage to carry six plates at once?" Andy asked in frank admiration.

"Here, Andy, I'll show you. You put one in this hand, another resting on the wrist, but overlapping the first a bit, the third balanced up higher on your — uh oh."

"What's the matter?"

"Your arms aren't long enough."

"So how do I carry six plates at once?"

"You ask me for help."

Andy laughed. "Okay, Steve. Help! I've got six hungry customers across the room."

"At your service," he told her, carrying the plates for her.

In the kitchen, Ina Cord was running at a frantic pace. Maybe it was the wonderful smell of the chili penetrating the neighborhood, but the crowd tonight was much bigger than they'd been expecting. At the cash register, that was good news, but in the kitchen, it was bedlam. She was extremely grateful for Toby and the basketball players, all of whom were taking turns helping make batches of chili. It was selling almost faster than they could make it, too.

"Onions! I'm out of onions. Tex, go get me some. No, no! Don't stop cutting up the beef. Get someone else to go down. Andy knows where we store the onions. Somebody go get her. Or Steve. He knows, too. Charlie, get Andy — or Steve. We're out of onions."

Charlie left the kitchen in search of Andy. One of the Texans went to look for Steve.

"Andy, Mom needs onions. She says you know where the back-ups are stored."

"Right, I do, Charlie," she told him. "You take over here. Table 18 is ready for coffee. Table 16 is dawdling, but they're going to want more chili in a minute. I'll be back soon."

"Okay, Andy. I can handle it."

Andy handed him her order pad and went to the door to the store room. The door, as usual, was locked. Andy took the key off the

hook, unlocked the door, and left it ajar behind her with the key in the lock. She felt for
the light switch and walked carefully down
the stairs to the cold storage locker.

Ever since she'd been a little girl, Andy had
especially liked this place. It was a walk-in re-
frigerator, filled with all the fresh fruits and
vegetables for the restaurant. Her mother
bought many vegetables fresh daily, but others
could be bought and stored in large quanti-
ties. The walls of the locker were lined with
shelves and on those shelves were hundreds of
pound of potatoes, onions, carrots, beets, gar-
lic, turnips — anything that could last for a
long time. In a separate locker, at a colder
temperature, the restaurant's meat was stored.
Then there was a third locker, colder still, for
frozen storage.

She retrieved a ten-pound bag of onions for
her mother and started up the stairs. As she
got to the foot of the stairs, though, there was
Steve.

"Andy, that you?" he asked in the darkness.

"Yes," she told him. "What are you doing
down here?"

"I came to get your mother some onions."

"Thanks, but I already got them."

"Here, I'll carry them for you," he said.

She handed the bag to him and they walked
upstairs. At the top, Steve stopped, waiting
for her. She looked at the closed door and
then at him, suspiciously.

"You got the key, didn't you?" she asked.

"No, you've got it, don't you?"

"Uh-uh." She shook her head. "I left it in the lock. That's why I left the door ajar."

"Andy," he said, "I've got some bad news for you."

"I was afraid you were going to say that," she said. "You didn't notice the key in the lock, did you?"

"Nope. And now the door is closed."

"And locked," she said.

"Oh, Andy, I'm sorry," he said, embarrassed.

"Don't worry, Steve," she told him. "Mom's hot for the onions. Someone else will be down here in a few minutes — even if it's a customer looking for the rest room."

"So what do we do in the meantime?" he asked.

"We take our break, and hope Charlie's doing a good job covering our tables. Come on, let's go back to the bottom of the stairs and sit down. We deserve some relaxation."

"Well *you* certainly do," he told her. "You're really something in the dining room."

"That all?" Andy was emboldened by their unexpected privacy.

"Huh?" Steve asked, confused.

"I mean, is the only thing about me that you like the fact that I'm a good waitress?"

"Well, I, uh — " Steve seemed out of words.

"It just seems that you and I work pretty well together, and I actually was hoping to get a chance to know you a little better. Now we have the chance." Andy could hardly believe she'd said that.

"You were?" Steve asked, surprised. Pleased.

"Yes, I was. Tell me what you like to do when you're not being a first-rate waiter."

"Well, I study a lot. I really want to succeed at my studies."

"What do you study?"

"I'm a musician — or at least hope to be. I study piano and violin."

"Really?"

"Sure, but I have to work a lot to pay for my rehearsal studio. I can't practice at home. For one thing, I only have a small piano and for another, it drives my mother's neighbors batty."

"I know what you mean about studio time. I want to be a ballerina. It's very hard to find the time and the place for my own practice."

"Ballet, really?" Andy nodded. Steve continued. "I love ballet. Always have. When I was a kid, though, it was easier for me to get to concerts than ballet. For a while I took ballet lessons, too, but a lot of guys on the block were teasing me about it being sissy. So I stopped."

"That's terrible," Andy said. She couldn't imagine anything worse than having to give up ballet. "You could start again, you know. There's nothing in the least bit sissy about ballet."

"Don't have to tell me that now. It's prob-

ably the toughest physical activity there is.
Actually, as it turned out, when I couldn't
take ballet, I started studying the piano. I
love that even more, so it all worked out."

"I went to the ballet yesterday — "

"Did you?" Steve asked. "What did you
see?" Then Andy began telling him about the
performance she'd attended with Jane. He was
as fascinated by her description as she had
been by the performance.

"You know," Steve said. "I know you're
going back to school soon, but maybe we
could get some tickets for the ballet for when
you come home at spring vacation. Would
you like that?"

"Steve, I'd like nothing better."

"Deal," he said offering his hand. She shook
it. He had a nice firm handshake, but warm
at the same time. His clasp on her hand lin-
gered pleasantly. Then, on impulse, Andy
asked Steve the question she most wanted to
know.

"Steve, how come you've been so hard for
me to talk to?"

"I was going to ask you the same question,"
he said. "But I didn't want to embarrass you.
After all, you *are* the boss's daughter."

"I never thought of it like that," she told
him.

"And I never thought of it any other way,"
he confessed.

Just then, the door above them opened.

"Hello?" Andy called.

"Hey, Andy!" It was Charlie calling. "Where have you been?"

"Locked in the cellar. Have you come to rescue me?"

"Us," Steve corrected her, helping her to her feet and carrying the onions. "But to tell you the truth, Andy, I suspect we got rescued by being locked in here in the first place."

"I think so, too." She smiled at him.

CHAPTER
SIXTEEN

It turned out that the Texans were as comfortable on a dance floor as they were on a basketball court — and as happy, too. Their effervescent good spirits were positively contagious. Within minutes after the music began, they had every able-bodied person in the restaurant up and dancing.

"I've never seen anything like it," Mike Cord told Andy.

"Me, neither, Dad. Isn't it wonderful?"

"I'll say. Ten people have already made reservations for *next* New Year's Eve."

"We'll have to get the Texans stranded in Chicago again — "

"Maybe we can arrange something," Mr. Cord said, laughing.

Just then, Steve came up to them.

"May I have the pleasure of this dance?" He asked Andy. She nodded and smiled, tingling with excitement. As he swept her onto the dance floor, Andy wondered how she could ever thank her mother for running out of onions at *just* the right time. No, there was no way to explain. She and Steve began dancing then.

He was a wonderful dancer. So was she. Her knowledge of ballet and his of music combined beautifully as they twirled on the dance floor until they were each out of breath. She hoped the next dance would be a slow one. A very slow one.

"Come on, Jane," Bob the Lobber told her. "Let's dance."

"Hey, I don't know anything about country dancing," Jane protested.

"It's like making chili," he drawled. She looked at him, puzzled. "Not knowing how doesn't matter," he said.

"It doesn't?" she asked suspiciously.

"Nope. Because I don't know how to dance either. I think the trick is for me to keep my feet off of yours, right?"

"Sounds good to me," she said, laughing. "Let's give it a try!"

He held her around the waist and led her to the dance floor. As soon as they began dancing, Jane knew he'd been teasing her. He was a fine dancer — such a good one that it didn't matter that she didn't know what she was doing. She just followed him.

"Oops," she said. "I think it turns out that the trick is for me to keep *my* feet off of yours. I don't want you to return to Texas without any toes."

"No problem. My feet were an inch or two too big, anyway," he told her, straight-faced.

Toby stood near the kitchen, watching the dancers, listening to the music. She loved it all. It was like home, but it was different. The same, but not the same. It was fun. Texas in the Windy City. She laughed to think what her father would think of such a gathering.

"Say, Toby." It was Charlie.

"Yes?"

"Telephone for you."

"For me?"

"That's right. It's person-to-person."

Toby was nervous as she went to the phone. She couldn't imagine who would be calling her.

"Hello?" she said, picking up the phone.

"October Houston?" the operator asked.

"Yes, ma'am."

"Toby, that you?"

"Yes, it is. Who is this, please? Is something wrong?"

"Whoa, take it easy, Toby. It's Neal. Neal Worthington. Remember me?" Of course, she remembered him. She also remembered what Jane had told her about what he had said about her.

"Sure, we played tennis together at Canby Hall."

"I hope we'll have a chance to play again," Neal said.

"Not in *this* weather," Toby protested.

"Nope. We can wait until spring for that. But I hope I won't have to wait until spring to see you again."

"Well, I'll be back at school tomorrow," Toby told him.

"That's what I was calling about, actually," Neal said. "Can I meet your plane? If you're arriving tomorrow afternoon, I'll have time to drive all three of you back to school. Then you and I could maybe have some pizza at Pizza Pete's."

Toby couldn't really believe this was happening to her. But she certainly wasn't going to argue about it. "It's a deal," she told him. "We're arriving at 4:20. This'll be my first trip to a restaurant I wasn't working in since I turned professional. It'll be interesting to watch someone else do the work at Pizza Pete's tomorrow."

Neal laughed. "I can just see you critiquing the service there. Maybe I'd better bring sandwiches, instead — "

"Oh, I won't embarrass you. Let's make it pizza."

"See you then."

"Yeah. And, uh, Happy New Year."

"Happy New Year, Toby," he told her.

She hung up the phone and then stared at it for a while, bemused. Neal Worthington *really* liked her.

"Toby! There you are."

Toby turned to see two Texes, PeeWee and Everest. "Hi, boys."

"Hi, indeed. High and low is where we've been looking for you. We've talked the band into playing 'Yellow Rose of Texas,' and we need you to dance with us."

"Us?"

"Well, after all, it's *our* song."

Suddenly Toby had a mental image of herself dancing with six gigantic Texans. It was such a silly picture that she couldn't remain solemn for long.

"Let's go, boys," she agreed, linking arms with them. "But I think we're going to have to find five more Texas women for the dance."

"No problem, Toby," Everest assured her. "After an hour and a half of that music, *everybody* out there's a Texan!"

"You know, I can believe that," Toby told him.

By quarter to twelve, everybody was ready for the New Year. Hats and noisemakers had been distributed to all the guests and staff and the countdown had begun.

Jane and Toby sat at a table with Dan and Buck, drinking sodas.

"I've never danced so much in my life," Jane said, exhausted.

"Me, neither," Toby agreed.

"And the night's not over yet," Buck reminded them.

"How can you guys keep going?" Jane asked in wonder.

"It's easier than basketball — "

"But you don't get fouled out?"

Buck and Dan laughed. "It can't be all that hard, though," Dan said.

"What do you mean?" Toby asked.

"Well, look at your friend, Andy. She's still dancing."

And she was. Steve and Andy were still on the dance floor, still obviously absorbed with each other.

"Well, she's nearly a professional dancer," Jane explained.

Buck smiled at her. "Look again," he suggested. "I don't think it's the years of training at the barre that's keeping her going tonight."

"I guess you're right about that," Toby agreed.

Fourteen minutes later, everyone in the restaurant was poised with noisemakers, waiting for the New Year's countdown. Mike Cord had set his watch very carefully earlier in the day, so they would be sure to celebrate at the exact moment of midnight.

"Thirty seconds now," he said, and there was a hush in the restaurant while all the partygoers linked arms in one large circle.

"Twenty seconds," Mr. Cord told them, looking closely at his watch. The band picked up their instruments, ready to play at midnight.

"Fifteen seconds," he said. Then "Ten. . . ." Everyone joined in the countdown.

"Nine, eight, seven, six, five, four, three, two. ONE! *Happy New Year!*"

Then everyone rattled noisemakers and blew horns and shouted. The old year was gone, the new one begun. Each person turned to kiss the person on either side. Everyone that was, except for Andy and Steve. They just kissed each other. That was enough for them.

Then the band began to play "Auld Lang Syne," while the guests sang and swayed to the music. It was the first time most of them had heard that song played with such a distinct country twang.

Outside, in the cold night, the fireworks began. The explosions punctuated the singing, hugging, and kissing at the party. Even though the people in the restaurant couldn't see the rockets, the sound reminded them that their celebration was being shared by everyone in the city — in the time zone, really. Somehow the universality of the celebration made the party at the restaurant seem all the more joyous.

"Isn't it wonderful?" Toby asked Jane.

"What, you mean kissing all the Texans?" Jane teased.

"You haven't kissed us all," Rebound Pete interrupted. "For instance, you haven't kissed *me*."

"Purely an oversight," she told him, giving him the opportunity, which he took.

"And me," Dan said.

"Oh, yes, I did. I remember," Jane told him.

"Shucks, I thought I could fool you."

"Thought I was just a dumb yankee, huh?"

"Nobody who packs twenty pounds of stuff into a fifteen-pound suitcase as well as you do is dumb," he said.

"Toby, are all Texans like this?" Jane asked.

"Just six that *I* know of," Toby replied.

"Six is enough," Jane said.

"Say, the band is starting to play some real music again. Ready to keep yourself on my toes, Jane?" Bob asked.

"Well, why not?" she answered, heading back to the dance floor with him.

A few hours later, everything was quiet. Almost everything.

Jane, Toby, and Andy had volunteered to put away the food, or what was left of it, and lock up the restaurant for the night. When they'd finished, Jane suggested that they sit and talk for a few minutes before going up to the apartment.

Andy flicked off the neon sign in the window and walked over to the table where her friends sat. "The sweetest sound in the world," she said, echoing her mother's remark earlier in the week.

"I don't know," Jane said. "Tonight, for Toby and me, it means the end of something."

"Like sore feet, you mean?" Andy asked.

"No, like the end of an interesting experience."

"Not that it was all fun and games, mind you," Toby said. "A lot of it was sort of like trying to saddle break a longhorn."

"In a china shop," Jane added.

"But it was worth it?" Andy asked.

"As far as *I'm* concerned, it was worth it," Jane said. "I learned a lot, not just about carrying trays. I learned a lot about friendship. Thanks to you two."

"You're welcome," Andy assured her. "Say, can you believe we'll be back in Room 407 tomorrow night?"

"Oh, yeah, and I forgot to tell you that Neal's going to meet our plane and drive us to school," Toby told them.

"How'd you learn that?" Jane asked.

"He called tonight. Wanted to invite me to 'dine' with him tomorrow night at Pizza Pete's. I almost can't wait."

"I *told* you he was interested," Jane said. "And I can't wait to see Cary. I feel so stupid, making all that fuss over Zach."

"And I can't wait until spring vacation," Andy said. They didn't have to ask what she meant. The glow on her face said it all.

"Will your folks hold our jobs until then?" Toby asked, mischieviously.

The friends dissolved into exhausted laughter.

It had turned out to be a Happy New Year, after all.

CHAPTER SEVENTEEN

After a week of sharing their lives with the Cords, it was hard for Toby and Jane to say good-bye. It was harder still for the Cords to say good-bye to their beloved Andy.

"Don't worry, Mrs. Cord, we'll take care of her," Jane assured her hostess.

"And, if she gets homesick, I'll just make her a batch of chili," Toby volunteered.

"Thanks, Toby," Mr. Cord said smiling.

"Come on now, roommates," Andy said, bringing the farewells to a close. "We've got to get going, or we'll never get to the airport on time. The plane's going to be booked solid, so I want to be sure we get good seats."

It was time for Jane's surprise. "No problem with that, ladies. We're traveling First Class."

"*You* may be traveling First Class, but I'm in Coach with cold sandwiches on stale bread. Perhaps you can have the stewards send a hot meal back to me."

"That won't be necessary," Jane assured them. Then she explained about the mix-up with her seat on the way out. "So when they offered me First Class upgrades, I knew how much fun we'd all have together. Won't it be great?"

They all agreed on that.

Then the girls hugged all of Andy's family. Somehow, as hard as the week had been for all of them, saying good-bye was harder. Toby and Jane had come to feel a real part of this amazing family. It was an experience they would not soon forget. They promised to return to Chicago — if not to blue uniforms — and the Cords promised to come visit at Canby Hall.

Mike Cord drove them to the airport. He actually had two missions there. He was meeting the plane Elaine and Robert were on, coming in from their honeymoon in Jamaica. "If they don't get off that plane, you girls can just stay on a couple of days, can't you?"

"No!" they answered as one. "This has been wonderful, Mr. Cord," Toby told him. "But it's time us little dogies got ourselves back to school."

"Oh, all right," Mike Cord relented, teasing. "But I don't know who's going to dump food on my customers now that you all are gone — "

"You'll just have to find someone new," Jane said, knowing that he meant the gibe affectionately. "Perhaps you can retrain Robert and Elaine. . . ." Mr. Cord laughed out loud.

Andy and Jane were in the aisle seats. Toby sat by the window, next to Andy. Shortly after take off, they began to enjoy all the benefits of First Class.

"Would you care for something to drink?" the flight attendant asked politely.

"Yes, please, I'll have a ginger ale," Andy told her.

"And will you be having dinner with us this afternoon?"

"Oh, yes, indeed," Andy said.

When the stewardess had taken all their drink and dinner orders, she placed a white linen tablecloth on each of their tray tables for dinner and then moved on to the next row. The girls began talking.

"You know, I never used to think about how much work people do for you, everywhere," Jane remarked. "I sort of took it for granted, never even noticed it."

"No longer, huh?" Andy asked.

"I'll notice it from now on," Jane said. "I think a week's worth of work in your father's restaurant has taught me a *lot*."

"I know what you mean," Toby chimed in. "But it wasn't just what I learned at the restaurant."

"So what are your New Year's Resolutions?" Jane asked Andy.

"You asked first, you go first, Jane. Tell us

your resolutions. I bet they're interesting."

"Sure. Actually, I always make exactly the same resolutions for the New Year," Jane said.

"And you never fulfill them?" Toby asked.

"Oh, it's not that at all," Jane told her.

"Well, what are they?" Andy asked.

"Number One is to stop smoking. Number two is to stop biting my finger nails. Number three is to practice piano very thoroughly before each lesson.

"But Jane," Andy protested. "You don't smoke and you certainly don't bite your fingernails," she said, frankly admiring Jane's beautifully shaped and manicured nails

"And you don't take piano lessons," Toby added.

"See, I'm perfect!" Jane told them. "Here we are, sixteen hours into the New Year and there's almost no chance that I won't fulfill my resolutions. The year is guaranteed to be a success!"

Andy and Toby couldn't help laughing at Jane. She constantly amazed them.

"You know, Jane," Andy said. "I can understand Zach not realizing that you were wealthy. Most people expect wealthy people to be snooty, and you're not snooty at all. What I don't understand is that Zach didn't like you for what you *are*, which is wacky and wonderful — and best of all, our friend."

"Thanks, Andy," Jane said. "Actually, though, I'll confess to you two that I do have one New Year's resolution. It has to do with being honest with myself. When I got to the airport yesterday, I had a good long chat with myself, the first in almost a week. I'd been kind of avoiding *me*."

"We were mighty glad to have the real you back," Toby told her.

"Thanks," Jane said. "Okay, that's enough confessing on my part. Andy, what are your New Year's Resolutions?"

"While you are being more honest with yourself, I'm going to try being more honest with others. I wasted a lot of good time not telling Steve I'd like to get to know him better."

"You going to make up that time?" Toby asked.

"Yes, but we have to wait until spring vacation," Andy told them. "We'll be going to ballets and concerts together a lot."

"Swell," Toby moaned. "We're going to have to go two and a half months listening to Andy's anticipation of the next vacation's cultural events, just like it was before Christmas."

"Oh, I promise I'll be better this time."

"How?" Jane challenged her.

"This time I won't talk about the ballets and concerts, I'll talk about the boy who's taking me to them!"

"Some improvement," Jane teased. Andy just smiled to herself.

"And you, Toby," Jane asked. "What are your New Year's Resolutions?"

"I guess they have to do with what I discovered on my walk with Nancy, the time I got lost and had to find someone on a horse to help me. I want to try to break some habits I've got."

"Like nail-biting?" Andy asked her.

"Nope. No, I mean habits like thinking everything in Texas is the way the whole wide world should be. A week in Chicago taught me that's a silly attitude."

"How about the semester at Canby Hall before that?"

"Then, too, but somehow it sunk in more in Chicago."

"Must be the cold weather," Andy suggested.

Toby and Jane stared at her.

"No," Toby said. "I think it was getting lost and learning that what works in Texas doesn't necessarily work in Chicago."

"But it *did* work," Jane reminded her. "The man on the horse *did* save you."

"That was luck. I know I can't count on luck. I have to be able to count on myself. See?"

Andy and Jane did understand.

Then their dinners were delivered. They each had a fresh crisp green salad and a sizzling hot steak, with baked potato and green beans. The flight attendant went on to serve the other people in the First Class cabin.

"This is great," Toby said in undisguised joy. "I never traveled this way before."

"Oh, I don't know how great it is." Jane began mimicking one of her fussy customers. "I wanted mine medium-rare, but you know, not so much rare as medium, like he wants his more rare than medium. And *my* baked potato should have chives, but not sour cream, like hers, but with extra butter. And instead of the green beans, I was hoping for some peas. Do you have some, but without any of the mushrooms in them? And skim milk, honey? I'm watching my waistline."

By the time Jane had gotten to the skim milk request, Andy and Toby were laughing so hard they couldn't swallow their food.

"My greatest New Year's Resolution is never, I mean *never* fail to appreciate good service in a restaurant," Toby said.

"With a big tip?" Andy suggested.

"A very big tip," Toby assured her.

Just then, the attendant came by with a tea pot.

"Would you like some tea?"

"Yes, please, ma'am," Toby said politely.

"And some cream puffs?"

"Thank you," Toby nodded. When she had been served, she turned to Jane and Andy. "First Class is wonderful, you know. Based on this experience, I'm pretty sure I could break some of my old habits and learn to love a life of idle wealth." Andy nodded in agreement.

"Just one problem with that, though," Jane warned her friends. They looked to her for an explanation. "There's no such thing as First Class at Canby Hall."

"Oh, yes, there is," Toby corrected her. "There's First Class friendship and you can't ask for anything better than that!"

Jane and Andy nodded in agreement. Even in the roughest times, the roommates knew they had each other. Andy lifted her teacup in a toast. Toby and Jane reached for theirs as well.

"To friendship," Andy said.

Clinking teacups across the plane's aisle, Toby and Jane echoed her.

"To friendship!"

When Jane's family throws a party, Jane is counting on her roommates to be there. But what if Toby and Andy can't handle a night in Boston high society? Will they lose a friend forever? Read The Girls of Canby Hall #22, PARTY TIME.